Don Moore was born in Montreal and graduated from the Montreal Graphic Arts Technical Foundation in 1979. His talent and dedication led him to Nova Scotia that same year, where he worked in Graphic Arts for an impressive 36 years. Don received the Nova Scotia 2001 Woodland Owner of the Year award for sustainable forestry practices and was featured in forestry books. His exceptional talent in wood art has been showcased through commercials and television and has been acknowledged with the prestigious Master Status by Nova Scotia Art. In 2023, Austin Macauley published Don's *Memories of A Kid from the Heights*.

I want to express my gratitude to the members of the Mi'kmaq Nation who welcomed me to attend various cultural activities at their center, where I was introduced to their customs and beliefs, including drumming circles and journeying.

Don Moore

# TWO KEYS TO ENTER A PARALLEL WORLD

AUSTIN MACAULEY PUBLISHERS®

LONDON * CAMBRIDGE * NEW YORK * SHARJAH

**Ordering Information**
Quantity sales: Special discounts are available on quantity purchases by corporations, associations, and others. For details, contact the publisher at the address below.

**Publisher's Cataloging-in-Publication data**
Moore, Don
Two Keys to Enter a Parallel World

ISBN 9798891557604 (Paperback)
ISBN 9798891557611 (ePub e-book)

Library of Congress Control Number: 2024916228

www.austinmacauley.com/us

First Published 2024
Austin Macauley Publishers LLC
40 Wall Street, 33rd Floor, Suite 3302
New York, NY 10005
USA

mail-usa@austinmacauley.com
+1 (646) 5125767

Thanks to Dr. Zalman Amit's dedication and encouragement, this manuscript was edited and is now in production fulfillment.

# Table of Contents

# Prelude

I want to clarify that my book is a work of fiction inspired by my involvement in my shamanic journeying experiences and my close friendship with native Mi'kmaq. Although the book deals with an arms-length subject of some indigenous culture, I do not have any native ancestry. The indigenous culture I draw inspiration from is the Mi'kmaq Nation, known for its rich spiritual practices and deep connection with nature. The primary goal of this novel is to share some of the lessons and insights I have learned through personal life experiences and exposure to shamanic journeying.

It takes time and effort to develop a solid moral compass. Unfortunately, these principles cannot be instilled before birth. The first five years of our lives are crucial for physical, intellectual, and socio-emotional development. This book, which explores the themes of personal growth and shamanic journeying, follows the journey of young Kenja (Anthony is his given name) as he grows into adulthood and subtly highlights various morals and philosophies. Sometimes, these are directly brought to awareness, while others are obscured.

Despite a tragic beginning with the untimely loss of their parents, Kenja and Teddy's ten-year upbringing with their grandparents in Witchenbrook, outside the Osaken People's properties, brought a new level of awareness and opportunity to Kenja's life. During his formative years, he was immersed in various native teachings from his grandfather's perspective, balanced by the many influences from his non-native grandmother. This delicate balance in life continued into his young adult years as he delved into shamanic journeying at the Culture

Center, trying to establish a link between his hockey coaching career and social life.

Kenja's life was severely impacted when his beloved Grandmother Dawnlilly passed away, suddenly uprooting him from his known neighborhood and young friends and exposing him to an entirely different world, one that was painfully challenging. As time passed, Kenja's brother Teddy started to thrive in their new home and surroundings, located in a city that primarily white people inhabited. He became fixated while more at ease with his new environment.

Teddy didn't just attend school. He devoured it. He consumed information like a ravenous cheetah, seemingly with no limit to what he could absorb. While gaining entry to Harvard Medical School was no easy feat, it was not impossible or left unchallenged. Teddy entered Harvard with eagerness, determination, and one objective in mind. He emerged as Dr. Edward Rodgers, a neurosurgeon from Harvard's hallowed halls, a testament to his unwavering dedication and hard work.

# The Jazz Band

I was a young boy lying on my favorite blanket in my bedroom as the sunlight beaming through a window warmed me while listening to the steady beat of my grandfather's drum. As I fixated on the drumming, I was prepared to start my journey. It's something like a dream with intention. Sometimes, a journey might reveal a lesson; sometimes, it's about our morals, and as we age, some destinations and objectives follow suit. Your receptiveness becomes your compass as to where and why you journey.

As the rhythmic drumming slowly faded into the distance, I began my journey into a virtual parallel world. I descended into a rabbit hole cascading past a waterfall like a leaf on a calm autumn day. The serenity filled my nostrils with heavenly scents. I treasured these journeys into a parallel world with the insights and lessons encountered while meeting these circumstances and possibilities.

It was a good day for a walk for a young boy as I traveled a familiar path through this dense forest. There was so much to learn and see along with this old friend of a trail. With the warm sunshine keeping me company, this was a chosen day to journey.

A sudden gust of more than cool air challenged the warm breeze that accompanied me; there was a noticeable bitterness. A few gray clouds formed overhead, but the cynical black vision on the horizon was what was much more of a concern. I didn't have to see the Moose, realizing that death and destruction were on the march down the mountainside in its menacing parade.

I returned to the Lilly Pond, where I had passed about ten minutes before. There, I had stopped to enjoy these three frogs dressed in their tuxedos standing on a Lilly pad playing jazz. The sounds coming from the sax were nothing shy of majestic and blended so well while augmenting the piano and drums.

I felt agitated and out of breath as I reached the pond's bank. Noticing that the ice was unexpectedly forming on these warm temperate waters, the Moose had to be getting very close.

"Come with us!" cried the terrified frogs. Quickly, I scrambled across the water from Lilly pad to Lilly pad until I reached them. "Come on, dive with us, and be quick of it."

The ground was now trembling like a possessed earthquake, identifying the Moose's arrival at the pond's edge and the death it represented. I dove below the water's surface seconds before the forming ice abruptly thickened.

I followed the frogs deeper and deeper until we arrived at a tunnel where a rabbit anxiously awaited our arrival. It was a white rabbit; it was white until it started hopping, becoming a rainbow of colors. Saying a hurried goodbye to the Jazz Trio of frogs, we now seemed to be racing through a warren heading back to yesterday.

Suddenly, we found ourselves in this brilliant cavern containing tiny bunnies, the equivalent of a King's Palace. It was warm again, and the earth's trembling had ended. I needed to rest and felt comforted until this tap on my shoulder told me I had to return outdoors.

Looking out a window, I saw it was now pouring rain. It was not an ordinary shower but a very acidic rain, toxic enough to burn through and consume metal and glass. In the distance, there were these enormous toadstools. How were these toadstools able to survive and repel this acid rain?

"Time to go," said the rainbow rabbit. The King's Palace vanished, and I found myself under this huge toadstool umbrella, watching the acid rain devour everything.

Then I heard the drums, as the steadily increasing rhythm beckoned me to begin my return, to ascend from the rabbit hole. I want to follow the sound of these drums to safely return from my journey back to this existing parallel world. "Follow the drums; don't yield to the temptation to continue the journey, risking never to return." This critical shamanic directive was essential for all to respect, thus assuring one's safe return.

As I opened my eyes, I found myself lying on my blanket on the floor of my room. My grandfather asked if I remembered any details about my journey and what lessons I may have learned from the experience.

The re-entry can be an alarming shudder, and the fatigue factor associated was evident. It is essential to let your spirit and soul dictate the rate of return and the time needed.

My Grandfather WiKenja started almost inaudible drumming, clearing my mind of anything unnecessary.

"Grandfather, my lesson was that things are only sometimes as they appear."

"How was this revealed to you, Kenja?" My grandfather asked.

"As I witnessed the devastating effects of acid rain and narrowly escaped a dangerous moose, I began to doubt my teachings. Toadstools, being a type of fungus, had the potential to kill me, so how could they possibly save me? Nevertheless, I trusted in the wisdom you taught me, Grandfather, keeping in mind that things are not always as they seem."

"It was a good journey, Kenja. Tell me, where did the drumming first lead you?"

"To my mother's garden, Grandfather, through the ancestors' room. I followed the musical notes to the opening on the wall."

"Did you enter here?" Grandfather asked.

"Yes, once seeing the opening in the wall, I entered with the sound of the drumming."

"You haven't mentioned being in the presence of your power animal, the red-tailed hawk, your protector, Kenja; this is a steadfast rule regarding a safe return."

"If you do not respect the ways to journey, the journey will also not respect you, Kenja."

"Anyone can make a mistake once, a few a second time, and only the most determined a third time."

"Now rest your head and sleep easy, Kenja."

# The 'Mad' Journey

Our parents died from injuries sustained in a traffic accident when we were infants. Teddy and I survived, and because our father was an only child, as was our mother, the courts awarded us to the custody of our mother's parents, our grandparents. They raised us where our grandfather had resided from birth in the remote northern area of Ontario in Witchenbrook, outside of the Osakens Reserve.

For ten fun-filled years, I learned some of the ways of the Osakens, a few customs, beliefs, habits, and pearls of wisdom. Just as our Grandfather WiKenja gave his non-native wife Lilly her native name, Dawnlilly, he gave me my native name, Kenja. Teddy resisted receiving his native name so much that our grandfather made his native name Ted'dy.

While raised by our grandparents in this environment, I felt a connection to my grandfather's ancestry. On the other hand, Teddy nearly always seemed to manifest a protective shield preventing this culture from penetrating his spirit or soul. He never accepted, never let himself fit in, and remained secluded.

Grandmother Dawnlilly gave us unconditional love, trying to replace the loss of our mother, her daughter Dawn. I got to know my mother through my grandmother's stories and the inspirational teachings she shared with Teddy and me as she nurtured our upbringing. Teddy would overtly distance himself from these teachings. I felt for my brother Teddy and this situation he found himself in.

We received our formal education at the NCPS, Northern Community Public School, where Teddy felt the connection he needed by associating with many of the non-native students attending this school and the non-natives from the surrounding communities affiliated with this institutional learning center.

I am thankful to have had this time living with my grandparents. My grandfather always struck me as the wisest person in the world, and Grandmother Dawnlilly was a true blessing when she came into his life. Teddy and I were fortunate to have these two as our grandparents.

When WiKenja met Lilly at a High School Exchange Program in Morishburg, he just knew that this charming, beautiful white woman was to be his future soulmate. They built their home in an area where most couples comprised one native and one non-native couple. As he predicted, their life together flourished, blossoming as Lilly became Dawnlilly with the birth of their daughter Dawn, now completing the circle.

Whenever Dawnlilly hugged me, her warm embrace would melt away any negativity surrounding me, bringing me a sense of optimism, hope for the future, and a fresh start with the morning sun.

When I was nine years old, one of my fondest memories was always gazing at the horizon, anticipating the sunrise over the Osaken River in Witchenbrook at my grandparents' home just outside the boundaries of the Osaken Reserve while sitting on the weathered wooden steps of their house.

When my grandfather WiKenja, could join me, it made it special. I eagerly listened as he related some adventures when he was a young boy my age, noting how so many things have changed during these gone-by days.

"I thought I might find you sitting on the front steps waiting for a new day to begin, Kenja. Do you mind if I join you?"

I watched him grimacing while bending his knees, as his discomfort has become more noticeable lately.

"I would be disappointed if you didn't, Grandfather. I was thinking about some lessons I have learned from you and the ones I forgot during my last journey. And failing you, I wish I could have that day back and change things.”

My grandfather rubbed his forehead and remained silent for several moments before speaking.

“It is wise to admit to mistakes that we all make but unwise to wish them undone, allowing them to make another appearance, Kenja.”

As he spoke, I noticed my grandfather showing signs of aging as once he could easily squat comfortably, but not so today.

He spoke of his father, my great-grandfather KenWi, and how, during a poor day of fishing, he suggested returning the next day.

“I remember suggesting this to my father like yesterday, Kenja.”

“Perhaps, Father, if we leave today and return tomorrow, it might be a better day for fishing.”

A faint smirk on my grandfather’s face indicated that he had just remembered a meaningful distant memory.

My father replied, “We are fishing today.”

“If tomorrow should ever come, it will only again be today, so we might as well stay with the day we know exists, WiKenja.”

“The lesson, Kenja, teaches us that it is wiser to keep what we have rather than risk losing it in pursuing something better. The white man has an expression: *A bird in the hand is worth two in the bush.* This is an excellent lesson.”

“Hold onto your mistake, Kenja. It has passed without consequence, and you have learned from it.”

Slowly grasping the hand railing and again painfully rising, taking my hand:

“So, young Kenja, this is a fine morning well suited for a journey. Allow me to drum for your journey, and we can spend time together until your grandmother wakes.”

“Remember when I didn’t journey? I just fell asleep?”

That big grin on his face, the one that would light up a room, beamed widely.

“Oh, I remember that day, Kenja. It is not all that uncommon.”

"I will be sure to pass these things on to the family in my future, too."

His face perked up like a spooked deer.

"So, you are going to have a family, are you?"

"And so many questions from you this morning, Kenja. I'll have to tell your grandmother not to allow you to eat so much too close to your bedtime."

He placed my face in the palms of his hands.

Once more, Grandfather paused enough to ensure my full attention before continuing.

"Your red-tailed hawk is the spirit that helps guide and protect you, Kenja. So please heed these customs of our ancestors."

Then clapping his hands together:

"Remember this, Kenja, during your youth, experience the journey. Let them take you where they may."

I watched my grandfather prepare the sweet grass and sage to begin smudging me and my blanket and then himself and his drum, cleansing for my journey, a practice that hasn't changed for thousands of years.

I lay on my blanket while assuring the red-tailed hawk accompanied me as my grandfather's faint rhythmic drumbeat led me to my journey's entrance.

The porthole entrance could be anywhere, usually down a rabbit hole or other ground entrance.

At the start of this journey, I fell into an open cavity of a tree, tumbling down through the darkness and finally bumping into three sets of eyes looking at me in the darkness surrounding me.

"Hey, watch it, you klutz."

"What are you doing, and where did you come from with no manners, never mind good, but of any manners?"

"That's right, Willy, that's right? Very short, isn't he?"

"Isn't that right, Beau?"

"Well, he's not that short," said Forbsy. "Not for his age, I would think."

"How old is he, Forbsy?" Beau asked.

"He's old enough to have a name, and I've met younger people who dropped in on us who had a name." Willy shrugged.

"Excuse me, but I was only looking for an entrance to begin my journey. My name is Kenja, and who would you three be?"

As my eyes adjusted to the dim lighting inside this tree cavity, I noticed a rabbit, not the rainbow rabbit, but a brown one. Peering out from behind the brown rabbit was the face of a frog.

So, I asked the brown rabbit, "What is your name?"

"I am called Willy. Willy the Rabbit, thank you very much."

"And what is the name of the frog behind you, Willy the Rabbit?"

"His name is Beau, and he's not a frog. He's a beaver, Kenja."

"He sure looks like any frog I know, Willy the Rabbit."

"Get out from behind me, Beau, and show yourself to our new friend, Kenja."

"Hey, he's not a beaver. He's a frog in a fur coat."

"Well, he told us he was a beaver, and the fact that we had never seen a beaver before, we never questioned him about being a beaver. Then he told us he was a Canadian, so it's likely he could be a beaver, isn't it, Willy? Because all Canadians say, eh, right?"

"And Beau is always saying, eh. Also, he's very polite, like those Canadians."

Beau began saying,

"One day I woke up…"

Hesitating long enough for Willy the Rabbit to jump in, saying, "One day, one day, you woke up! Ha."

"Only one day, that's mad, isn't that mad, Forbsy?"

Forbsy echoed, "That's mad. Only one day."

"That's mad, Beau," repeated Willy the Rabbit.

"So, what did you do on all the other days you lived being this beaver impostor you seemed to be if you only woke up one day?" Forbsy asked.

I interrupt to try to enter the conversation.

"I could imagine I would only wake up one day too if I were a frog in a fur coat with deep emotional problems like our good friend, Beau, apparently has. It would be best if you were being seen by a doctor, Beau."

"That's mad," echoed Willy the Rabbit. "Isn't that mad, Beau?"

Looking at me, they both asked, "Are you making a house call, Dr. Kenja? Is that why you dropped in on us so unexpectedly? You certainly exhibit poor bedside manners, and your entry needs working on, too."

"That's mad," Chirped Forbsy.

"This whole day is becoming mad, isn't it, Beau?"

"We should go now, said Forbsy. I called a cab for us."

"That's mad, Forbsy. Who did you call?" Beau asked.

Forbsy responded, "I called Tilly the Turtle, and she'll be here any second now."

"Why Tilly the Turtle Forbsy?" Willy the Rabbit asked.

"I called Tilly the Turtle Willy the Rabbit because Beau is in a hurry to go and dam up the stream with no water," said Forbsy.

"You be sure to buckle up your seatbelt, Kenja because Tilly the Turtle is such a fast driver and is very concerned about the possibility of crashing. When she crashes, it's a gut-wrenching slow-motion mad crash, and they're the worst kind by constantly replaying in your mind, frame by frame, by frame," said the long-winded Forbsy without taking a breath.

"That's mad, echoed Willy the Rabbit."

I noticed Beau was carrying a flyswatter.

"What's with the flyswatter, Beau?"

Jumping in, "That's his Beavertail," Willy the Rabbit quipped.

"Isn't that mad?"

I could hear the drumming beckoning me home.

"You guys are a riot, a mad riot, but a riot just the same."

I was never so happy to hear the drumming calling me home and signaling the end of my journey. Suppose my grandfather asks me about lessons learned and experiences encountered on this one. In that case,

I'll tell him this was another time when I couldn't find my porthole to enter.

However, my favorite expression now is, "That's mad!"

# Becoming Aware

It has been said that you can't miss something that you have never experienced or are unaware of. I clearly remember the day when I was seven, and what was sorely missing in my life came thundering through the door.

It was one of those warm, rainy summer days when playing outdoors was limited due to so many lightning strikes in the area. Vince's mom made sandwiches for Little Buck, Vince, and me for lunch as we played indoors.

Vince's mom, Mary, was always so much fun. She enjoyed the chance to entertain three little seven-year-old boys. She started picking us up one at a time and swinging us around as we all laughed, watching each other get swung and tossed into the air. It was magical when it was my turn to have this experience; I was still unaware of this sense of being connected to a mother. My grandmother was no longer physically capable of doing the demanding things that Mother Mary did.

I watched as Mother Mary picked up Little Buck, who was little, so she could swing him higher than Vince or me. He was emitting this shrilling shriek and laughter, with tears running down his eyes.

It was very similar when it was Vince's turn until the swinging ended, and Mother Mary embraced Vince in a way that I had never seen nor been embraced. My Grandmother Dawnlilly would hug me, but not in the manner I was just exposed to. This seemed very different; it was not one I could describe, but undoubtedly one I could sense.

I always missed not having a mom, but until this moment, I was unaware of what I was missing. I watched Mother Mary beaming, showering Vince with the love only a mother possesses. Seeing this for the first time, I felt a change happening inside me, not a good change, an emptiness never realized before, of being abandoned and suddenly feeling all alone for the first time.

Being only eighteen months old, I never experienced the sudden, unexpected shock when a child loses a parent, especially a mother. The shock that young people who are old enough to realize what had happened never registered, but today, becoming aware of the love and bond between Vince and his mom brought on a numbness, an emptiness that I tried to shake off. Still, it clung to me like a shadow.

Mother Mary picked me up next, but it was no longer the same for me. It almost became repulsive. I was caught between needing this connection and not wanting to confirm that something was missing in my life, now recognized and registered. Once you realize something, you can't ignore it, and this realization impacted me.

Grandmother Dawnlilly would usually be the first to notice my anxiety building with the potential of demanding things from me that were not feasible for me at the time, still dealing with the sense of being abandoned with the death of my mother and father.

My grandmother thought that finding an outlet to express my inner feelings would help her understand and find a way to engage with them. When she noticed or sensed that I might be withdrawing again, she would escort me around the back of the house to her small workshop, her studio, where she would work on her various art interests, of which painting was indeed her gift.

Wordlessly, she would inevitably guide me there. Once inside, she would set out brushes, oils, and one of my grandfather's animal hides as my canvas. I sat quietly in the corner on her squatty little stool and waited until she motioned to me to come and reveal my inner thoughts or concerns on my canvas. These were the only words spoken before she went to sit in front of her easel.

"Don't think, Kenja. Paint."

This was always a short-term fix for me, getting me through the day or experience, but the root of my issues festered, taking its toll. Now that I was aware of what I had missed out on, the nurturing bond that a mother and child typically share, I noticed small things that never stood out; even how I was disciplined differed from how Little Buck and Vince were. The strictness and punishment weren't parent-oriented; something was lacking. These positive and negative memories are painful reminders of what could have been and what I missed out on.

I overheard my grandparents discussing their concerns regarding my steady, disruptive behavior and how inept they felt in dealing with my unforeseen awareness of the loss of my mother. Grandmother Dawnlilly expressed an urgent need to seek some outside professional help for me before I continued to fall further from the outward appearance of a stable, healthy life. When I heard my grandfather agree, acknowledging something had to be done and done soon. I again felt betrayed, becoming even more emotionally vulnerable.

I started to resent both Little Buck and Vince as each day would reveal more to me as to what I lost that day of the fatal accident that separated both Teddy and me from our parents and, in another way, separated Teddy and me by our very different coping processes. Teddy used any means to acquire knowledge as a method of coping or, in my case, lack of awareness nor any mechanism of deflection once I did become aware of my loss.

Teddy was nearly five years old on the day of that fatal crash that took our parents' lives and has appeared to deflect this loss by seeming to be able to use learning as a way to jam up this parental void from entering everything else, one that I could only assume he was experiencing. My issues soon carried over at school as I constantly began to cause disruptions, disruptions I would find out later were my yearning for attention.

The school authorities, councilors, and teachers met with my grandparents. Upon review of my actions and continued more aggressive disruptions, they suggested professional help was now paramount if this situation was to be corrected before manifesting itself, where my actions might ruin any chance of reversing this mental spiraling instability.

My grandparents sat me down and explained their concerns and the decision to find a corrective positive path for me. Grandfather spoke first.

"Kenja, we are unable to help or understand the reactions you have displayed since becoming aware of the loss of your parents and especially your mother; by ourselves, we are of little help to you."

Grandmother Dawnlilly continued, taking my hand while gently squeezing it.

"The loss of our daughter Dawn was so devastating for us, and we are still grieving her loss, but over time, we have found a means of coping, but nothing much more than coping."

"Our loss was immediate, Kenja. Your loss took years and a single incident to reveal itself, and it may not take years, but undoubtedly a good amount of time and with the right help to let you manage to cope with this concern for your well-being."

My grandfather walked me and my grandmother to the Witchenbrook train station, where we would board the train to Morishburg. So many new experiences for a seven-year-old in one day.

I'd never been on a train or even to the train station before, and heading for Morishburg for the first time added to my anxiety. We would meet Dr. Kuznetsov, a physiologist specializing in children's trauma. He was recommended by one of the school's administrators.

I was wound up tighter than my toy train, clinging to my Grandmother Dawnlilly. As we arrived, the train was waiting at the station, looking like a steel monster to me. Grandfather handed the tickets to my grandmother, and then said his goodbyes as we boarded the train.

Once aboard, I welcomed the warmth of the passenger car as the walk to the station was bitterly cold. With so many new things to look at, I began to relax more. Grandmother Dawnlilly sat quietly beside me as the conductor checked our tickets.

As we pulled out of the station, the train whistle sounded, and with a sudden jolt, the journey began. I knelt on my seat, looking out the window, catching glimpses of things as the train speed increased. This blurriness mimicked my life right now.

Grandmother Dawnlilly woke me as we approached Morishburg. It was dark outside, and all these lights and tall buildings were foreign to me. I retracted into a fetal position, clinging to my grandmother.

My grandmother grew up in Morishburg and attended the University of Morishburg, so she knew the city well. Although she mentioned that there had been many changes over the years, the basic layout of the area remained the same.

Grandmother asked for a taxi, and when it arrived, the driver greeted us, took our luggage, and put it in the trunk. Then he picked me up and jokingly said he should put me into the trunk, too. This action of being picked up and swung triggered a memory of the day Mother Mary's affection for her son Vince triggered what was missing in my life, causing me to react aggressively. My grandmother assured the driver he had done nothing wrong.

Grandmother registered us at the hotel, and a porter helped us to our room. I'd never been in an elevator before, and the sensation of ascending quickly triggered my vulnerability. Grandmother wisely decided it might be best to have room service deliver our evening meal to our room.

Dr. Kuznetsov's office was on the ninth floor of a Medical Arts Building. I'd never been in any building over two stories, let alone riding in an elevator for the second time. His receptionist, Jinsu, greeted us. She reminded me of Vince's mom, Mother Mary. She was just what I needed to feel a sense of comfort in these unfamiliar surroundings.

Dr. Kuznetsov was not nearly as foreign as his name suggested, not what I had envisioned in my seven-year-old mind. My grandmother and Jinsu walked me into a spacious room with a huge bookcase, and Dr.

Kuznetsov was reading a book. As the doors opened, he warmly greeted us, directing us to our chairs and asking if we would like refreshments. His voice was soft yet assuring, and his mannerisms were calming, positively affecting me and easing my apprehension.

I didn't talk much during our visit and wasn't encouraged to. Grandmother Dawnlilly answered the questions as the doctor took notes, occasionally checking for any reaction I might reveal. Grandmother explained that I went by two names: Anthony, my Christian, and Kenja, my native name given to me by my grandfather. I said I wasn't sure which name I preferred when he asked me.

He explained to my grandmother that when a child of six years of age loses a parent, particularly a mother, the first two years after losing a parent are a high-risk period for developing depression. In my case, only becoming aware of this loss at the age of seven and the disruptive behavior that followed is what often occurs at this point.

Our session lasted one hour, and my grandmother seemed pleased with how this initial meeting went. Looking back, I remember nothing about the day. I can only sense that I must have just found safety, withdrawing inwardly, becoming invisible.

We had supper in the hotel dining room before heading upstairs to our room. This was my first experience eating in a fancy place. Grandmother suggested using the word dining, and she showed me how to use the proper knife and what each of the spoons and forks was for. I concentrated so much on the utensils that I don't remember what I ate that night. Still, the experience was neat, and I couldn't wait to tell my grandfather all about it.

When we got into the elevator, Grandmother let me push the button for our floor. Once I was ready for bed, Grandmother talked with me, explaining that Dr. Kuznetsov would see us again tomorrow because we live far away. We would at first be in the room together, but if I felt comfortable, it would just be me and the doctor. I smiled at my grandmother, asking her if I could soak in the big bathtub with lots of bubbles.

When I got out, Grandmother wrapped me in the giant, fluffiest towel I had ever seen. Her hug was sincere, reminding me of what was missing in my life. I hugged Grandmother back, telling her I would be fine speaking alone with Dr. Kuznetsov tomorrow.

Jinsu greeted us with her warm smile as we entered the reception area. While waiting, my grandmother told me that Dr. Kuznetsov would ask me questions about my issues and other aspects of my life, like my family and school, so he could get to know me better.

After meeting Dr. Kuznetsov, my grandmother joined Jinsu in the reception area while I met with the doctor. After identifying the triggers of my awareness, struggles in school, and resentment toward kids with parents, Dr. Kuznetsov suggested that I draw my concerns. I told him my grandmother had me paint whenever I became overloaded. I'll never forget what he said: One day I'll catch up to Grandmothers.

While waiting at the train station, we went shopping, and I spotted a stuffed bear. I picked it up and hugged it, showing it to my grandmother. Bear was to become my go-to person for years to come.

We returned to our train platform and heard someone calling, "Lilly, Lilly McGuire."

My grandmother turned around and was showered with hugs. Barbara, an old university alumni was thrilled to meet again after nearly forty years. When Barbara found out we would be back in Morishburg every week for the next while, she insisted we stay with her during these visits.

My grandmother and I took train trips for several months so that I could attend my sessions with Dr. Kuznetsov. During these sessions, I learned strategies to deal with fear, particularly the fear of losing someone I loved, like my brother Teddy. Dr. Kuznetsov used play therapy to help me healthily process my loss, and it worked well. One day, I realized and shared it with Dr. Kuznetsov—that maybe my desire to journey was motivated by my search for my mother's love.

This was my last session with Dr. Kuznetsov as he felt the door to my next chapter in life was open, and I was up to the challenge, knowing that he would always be just a phone call away if needed.

# Grandmother Dawnlilly

I loved living with my grandparents in the community of Witchenbrook, just off the Oasken Reserve. They unknowingly gave me more freedom during my formative years than I probably would have had if my parents had survived that car accident. Severe discipline was not my grandparents' way or method of achieving respect while developing morals; their method was arm's length teachings.

I was lucky to learn the white man's ways and some native customs in elementary school in Witchenbrook, sharing these experiences with my friends Vince and Little Buck. The school had a balanced mix of Osaken kids and non-native students, resulting in less hate, not no hate, but less animosity.

I easily fit into one side of this mixed equation and Teddy into the other, and I was concerned for my brother. Although he was older than me by nearly three years, this age difference had no bearing on the fact that we didn't hang out or play together all that often. The main reason was that we looked through very different windows to see the world around us.

The only thing remotely related to our grandparents' practices for Teddy would be when he would find a dead animal showing no apparent reason for its demise, bisect it, and investigate the possible cause of death.

Teddy had little use for holidays or summer vacation, so he pleaded with our grandparents to let him attend the Northern Community Public School extended summer school program. This request was usually granted, pleasing everyone, especially the teachers at the school. You see, although Teddy was still in elementary school, he was undoubtedly the smartest kid in the entire school, including the high school.

My interests were elsewhere, very far elsewhere. Whenever a religious holiday rolled around, I would try to convince my grandparents that staying home from school would show my respect for their faiths and beliefs. Although I never succeeded, they often praised my creative approaches.

Working alongside my grandfather in his woodland, I also wanted to make a positive environmental contribution by transplanting some crowded saplings into a less crowded area.

Once you understand how the thawing of the winter frost expands soil particles around the tiny hair-type roots, aerating these young tree roots and making them far less susceptible to losing these minute roots while being uprooted for transplanting, this aeration looks like an Aero-Bar once you bite a piece of it. At least, this was my reasoning when I told Grandmother Dawnlilly why I needed an Aero-Bar as an exhibit for my tree-planting research project at school. Once more, she gave me credit for a nice try.

I remember being around eight and asking my grandfather to show me his tree-planting methods and asking, "When is the best time to plant a tree?"

His response was quick and to the point, as he laughingly said, "Twenty-five years ago."

During the first year, I worked alongside my grandfather, learning and understanding some of nature's ways. In the following years, I was alone, expanding my fascination for forestry practices. My grandmother said that I loved trees so much that she feared that any day now, I would start to name them.

My grandparents had a good-sized vegetable garden, which they tended together until the plants were established. Then, it was left up to my grandmother, leaving my grandfather to concentrate on the more never-ending maintenance issues that cropped up around home.

Grandmother Dawnlilly was a honey producer who kept several beehives, often inspecting them using a smoker around noon. This was always better done on a clear and calm day when the sun was directly overhead, making it easier to see into the hive. Often, this is when the bees would be out searching for nectar and pollen.

My grandmother tended to her flower gardens as much as she would tend to her vegetable garden. I could understand this attention to the vegetables with the return during the fall harvesting. Still, for me, she was wasting her time and energy tending those flower beds. They looked okay, but you can't eat flowers.

It's always been a mystery to me how my grandmother could read my mind, but she seemed to be able to do so more often than not.

"Do you ever wonder why I maintain my flower gardens as much as my vegetable garden, Kenja?"

What! How did she know that? Maybe I talk in my sleep, or perhaps this is the women's intuition my grandfather keeps talking about. Sometimes, she freaks me out with her insights or whatever they are.

"No, not really, Grandmother. Okay, maybe sometimes, a little bit. But not that often."

"Why?"

"You know, Kenja, we could go hungry without the flowers for years."

Whoa, there must be more to this flower-growing thing than I thought.

"Sorry, I don't see the logic, Grandmother. Flowers won't sustain us, will they?"

"No, they won't be able to do that, Kenja, but the bees will need energy from the flowers to survive and reproduce by producing honey in their hives."

"If the bees should ever fail in numbers to adequately service the vegetables and the fruit trees needing cross-pollination, we could be in a sorry state of affairs, Kenja."

"So, Grandmother, no bees, no food?"

"That's a bit of a stretch, my little Kenja. Perhaps not actually 'no ' food, but if we are not mindful enough regarding the Bee's future, their future is also our future, Kenja."

I spent the remainder of this day helping my grandmother tend to her gardens and watching the bees constantly gather nectar and pollen, now with more respect for them.

After eating and cleaning off the table, as usual, Teddy and I washed and dried the dishes. I continued thinking about this day and my grandmother's lesson about respecting nature's balance.

I returned to the small outbuilding behind the house, which my grandmother used as her art studio. I wanted to thank her for taking the time from tending her gardens to spend with me.

Ode to Grandmother Dawnlilly

*When is the right time*
*To tell you how I feel*
*Every time's the right time*
*When it's Honest and it's Real*

*You taught me how to Treasure Life*
*How precious each one is*
*You taught me all there is to Life*
*And all the Spirit gives*

*You taught me that flowers matter*
*Just as much as trees*
*You taught me the Creator sees*
*The merit of the Bees*

# Coexisting Societies

My previous life and world seemed so distanced today while dealing with the hustle and noise-polluted life of the modern twenty-first century and the ever-changing technology accompanying this existence.

Anthony is my Christian name, Anthony Rodgers, my handle in the outside world where I work and live, existing as a hockey coach in a junior League, a job I love, striving to make it to coaching in the big time, in the major leagues.

My adopted family didn't value a coaching position as an actual career or occupation like that of a lawyer, engineer or, as my brother Edward, a doctor. Teddy was the firstborn; I am sure, taking most of the available brain cells in our mother's womb. Maybe I was nearly as intelligent as Teddy, but I never possessed the academic ambition he owned.

When our Grandmother Dawnlilly succumbed to illness, it was inevitable that we would no longer be allowed to live with our aging Grandfather WiKenja in Witchenbrook. The authorities soon had us placed for adoption. I feared Teddy and I would be separated through the adoption process and began to withdraw inwardly. Teddy was my older brother, and he was everything to me. If our separation happened, I would lose the only connection to our parents that I would have ever had.

Trusting our grandparents' instincts, I believed that Teddy's and my journey together was inevitably destined. Ultimately, this proved to be the case, as we were adopted as brothers by two amazing people, a loving couple named Faith and Donald Brooke. Our upbringing would now continue in the metropolis of Morishburg, Ontario—a definite cultural shock for me, an embracement for Teddy.

I'll never forget our adopted dad saying that trouble would surely follow with a name like 'Donnie Brooke'. I liked my new dad, Donnie Brooke. I had difficulty calling them Mom and Dad. The connection never existed for me, whereas Teddy was elated to do so.

Teddy flourished in his new environment, and his brilliance was evident in his academic achievements. He deserved all the praise, and I was very proud of my older brother and his accomplishments.

Teddy and I were so different. Some days, I wondered if it would have been better if they had separated us during our adoption. If this occurred, I would find a quiet place, letting these thoughts evaporate. I could never imagine my life without Teddy.

When we were still in high school, Teddy could disassociate from me to the point that most people didn't even know we were brothers. We certainly didn't resemble one another.

Teddy kept any semblance of his native background deeply buried. In contrast, I always spoke of my life shared with our grandparents Dawnlilly and WiKenja in Witchenbrook. I have always continued to use these experiences and teachings in my everyday life, and thinking back to today. Maybe I should have related more about my father's Irish ancestors. Of course, I never knew my mother or father, being an eighteen-month-old infant when that fatal car accident ended their lives. Dad didn't have much of a family tree to explore as an only child, and we had lived with our mom's family, covering all the possible family connections.

Often at school, I would be on the wrong end of a fist that someone threw toward my face because, in this predominantly white neighborhood, anything other than being of white Anglo-Saxon ancestry was not popular. Teddy often witnessed these fights but seemed to look the other way, Teddy being Teddy. Regardless, he was my brother, and I loved him.

Then, one day, Teddy messed up, and I mean messed up big time when I was still in junior high, and Teddy was in his final year of high school. Our adoptive parents had gone to see a stage play at the Morishburg Classical Theater of the Arts. We were on our own for the night, given money to order a pizza for supper, supposedly keeping us out of trouble.

After we ate, as usual, Teddy said he would study, so I called him my nerdy brother because he was my nerdy brother. I knew it bothered him whenever I called him nerdy.

Knowing I could outrun him, I bolted for the garage door to where my bike was, but he was too close behind me, and he would have caught me if I had tried to get it.

Teddy knew my bike was my prized possession, so he stopped and took it outside to the driveway. I wasn't sure what he would do because riding a bike wasn't something he ever did. Anything most boys would do, Teddy avoided it like the plague. If you couldn't read it, Teddy had little use for it.

"What are you going to do now, Mr. Nerd?"

"Walk my bike around the block?"

"Because I know that you certainly can't ride one."

Teddy didn't react the way I thought he would. I don't think he acted the way Teddy might have intended to do. Maybe it was the pressure he felt in his final year of senior high school and our adoptive parents' near-impossible expectations imposed on him. Still, his reaction was very out of character.

He hopped on the bike, undoubtedly the first time he had even thought about riding a bike, let alone doing it. He started peddling, quickly losing control of his balance. The bicycle now seemed to have a mind of its own. It turned left, heading for our adoptive father's classic 1957 Studebaker Golden Hawk, which he had painstakingly rebuilt himself.

Teddy came so close to avoiding hitting the car, but not quite close enough, resulting in a long scratch, no, more like a deep pronounced scrape peeling paint away, exposing bare metal, starting at the passenger door and not stopping until the bike passed the headlights.

Holly crap! This mishap was not going to end well at all. If this were a movie, the next scene would undoubtedly focus on a murder in Morishburg before this night played out. The number of hours our adoptive father spent searching for many elusive parts over the years was staggering. Let alone the labor of love he devoted, and the satisfaction of returning this classic car to its former beauty had bolstered his pride in doing so. We thought it best to remain outside waiting for our parents' return because, at that moment, it felt much safer not to be confined.

By the look in our adoptive father's eye, facial expression, and body language, we were all but assured that the punishment would be severe. Teddy would soon be writing his final exams and needed to ace all of them for acceptance into the Harvard Medical School in Boston. He had no time for any punishment, none.

I stood in front of Dad, looked him squarely in the eyes, and said that I was the one who had driven into the side of his car and that I was sorry for being stupid again. Under similar situations, it wouldn't be a stretch to accept my confession, and it would be the truth. As expected, the punishment would be long and harsh, even for Donnie Brook. Teddy tried to intervene, so I started arguing loudly, cutting him off.

When we were alone, Teddy asked me why I had admitted his lack of judgment. I told Teddy that while waiting for our adoptive parents to return, I had time to analyze the various options and their costs to either of us.

My confession would be far less consequential than his owning up to this accident. I told Teddy about one of our grandfather's lessons regarding values. The value of a beggar receiving a dollar from a poor man and this same dollar from a rich man would represent a very different contribution value from each donor.

"Teddy, you can live your dream of becoming a doctor. It surely has been your fate in life, but Harvard is not an easy entry, and the next few months will be the most critical for this possibility ever to become a reality."

Teddy stood there with his shoulders drooping, his long arms hanging lifelessly. This time, I took his face in my hands as I had watched our grandfather do so often garnering attention:

"And, Teddy, you better become the best damn doctor after this. I believe in you."

That same day, Teddy phoned our grandfather to apologize, regretting the missed opportunities and misplaced actions he had taken so many years ago.

But today, that's all ancient history. Teddy's hours of being a nerd paid big dividends as he graduated near the top of his class at Harvard Medical School. Today, I only wanted to do what they taught me to do. To live for today, live in the 'now'. But, as I saw myself, not to my adopted parent's image of me.

In our younger days, I would go journeying with our grandfather. It helped build my character and kept me connected to my present and the past and how, at this very moment, I longed for those days today.

Whenever I drove to the arena, I would try to leave my troubles at the door, but not always successfully. I loved the coolness of the arena, which may have resulted from growing up in the North Country. Hockey allowed me to spend much of my life in a fresh, crisp environment, and hockey, in a way, mimicked life, for you never really knew the score until the end of the game.

Circumstances abound during our lifetime, often dictating or simply offering a fork in the path that we are following. I would have never been exposed to hockey if not for my grandmother dying at a relatively young age, necessitating Teddy and my adoption, relocating us to a different environment within the limits of a metropolitan city where hockey ruled the day.

These memories from living with my Grandfather WiKenja gave me the opportunity to insert some of his wisdom into my hockey coaching career. I learned that survival, or in the case of hockey, winning, was more probable when you could envision where things would be, not just where they are at the moment.

It is late September, and the start of the hockey try-out season is upon us. Young hopefuls are flooding into the arenas with visions of making it to the NHL in their respective futures. I find that the guys who put all their effort into only concentrating on being selected at this junior try-out level, no further along the road to professional success, become the ones to continue to the next level in achieving their ultimate goal.

Looking back on my younger days when a seemingly trivial incident-slipping on an icy patch on a sidewalk had ultimately ruined any prospect for me making the NHL draft. How easily today I relate to these young prospects' aspirations and desire to break into the line-up at this junior level and have the opportunity to move on to the big show.

You have to excel, given the time and effort required and the ever-changing learning process of developing the skills and assets required to be considered for a spot on a hockey team in North America, even at the junior level, let alone the elusive NHL in this twenty-first century of modern international hockey players vying for a career.

Before my grandmother Dawnlilly passed away, and I still lived in Witchenbrook, my best friends Vince and Little Buck and I had never even played ball hockey, never mind ice hockey. Sure, there was international flag-waving support for Team Canada and a basic interest in the NHL in the community. Still, soccer was the primary sport for the area's young people. It was much less expensive for the needed equipment, and the community never had the support nor could ever afford to build even a basic indoor arena.

When Teddy and I were relocated through adoption to Morishburg to live with our adopted parents, Faith and Donald Brooke, hockey was one of the many exposures I faced with this relocation, one that was 180 degrees from my entire known being up to this point.

Once more, this sense of being abandoned and marooned on an island in the middle of life was more than just difficult for me to handle. But the thought of returning for therapy was to be my catalyst to find something, anything that would get me through this enormous wave that seemed intended to drown me once again.

In school, I didn't fit in or want to fit in unless I could be myself, never accepting other people's versions or expectations of me. Teddy was smart enough to know this fact that I would become hardened and introverted, averting any possible brotherly association between us. Looking back, Teddy was absolutely right; anything else would have been a significant deterrent to his ambitious goals in the medical world.

In life, we often step through a door that sometimes opens to new and unexpected opportunities; I had two classes remaining before the lunch break, both subjects I had worked well into the night to complete the essays. While getting my books and assignment papers from my locker, someone punched me in the back of my head, sending me my books and assignments to the floor. Big Bozo and his buddies picked up my assignments, thanking me for doing their work for them.

That was the moment I met my next best friend, Wayne Weir.

"Looks like you're making friends with the wrong people there, Buddy."

"Hi, I'm Wayne, what's your name?"

Feeling the lump on the back of my head, I opted not to use Kenja.

"Hi, Wayne, I'm Anthony. Thanks for helping me pick up my books. That big retard will get his one day."

"He's not worth your effort, Anthony. Besides, I don't think he'll be hassling you anymore."

And so our friendship began. It wasn't an immediate or best-friend kind of friendship. Still, once we started hanging out together, Wayne's physical presence alone would be intimidating enough that Big Bozo and company decided to find a new source to bully, resulting in less frequent scraps involving me.

"Anthony, a bunch of my teammates and I have access to the arena for some pick-up hockey early Saturday morning before they clean the ice with the Zamboni to start the day. We'll have the ice from 5:00 a.m. until about 6:30 a.m. Why don't you come along, too?"

"Naw, I don't think that would be a good idea, Wayne."

"Listen, most of my friends call me Wayner, okay? And why don't you come, Anthony."

There was no longer a need to delay to reveal that I couldn't skate. I never tried to skate, ever. I never had any interest or opportunity.

"What, you can't skate? You are a Canadian, right?"

"Then you can skate, eh! And I promise you that you will learn to skate, Anthony."

"You only need some help starting."

I started skating with Wayne and some of his teammates while holding onto a chair for balance, and within the hour, Wayner had me skating freely, still next to the boards, but on my own. I don't know how many times you can fall before breaking something, but I'll bet I was getting pretty near the required number.

Wayne was a skillful hockey player, skating with speed and a tremendously accurate shot. His physical size allowed him to shake off some of the physical abuse some lesser-skilled players have to rely on as being a team enforcer.

I took to hockey like a duck to water, and everything was now focused on achieving the skills needed to become a future Junior A League prospect. My grandfather always said, "If you're going to dream, you might as well dream big." And this was one of those times.

Then came the biggest surprise for me: when my adopted dad found out about my interest in hockey, he fully supported me; that was as long as my adopted mom was kept in the dark. He said we have to be sure that Faith, the Warden of Everything, didn't find out about it.

He gave me an area behind the finished Rec Room inside the utility room. The ceiling height was over ten feet, the width was twelve feet, and the length was over thirty feet; it was ideal for a hidden practice area where I could gain accuracy and strength with my shooting. Faith would rather be seen dead than ever enter this utility area, making it ideal.

I also learned that Donnie Brooke was a University of Toronto Rowing Club Team member with years of training background, which he eagerly shared with me.

Between the encouragement and help from Wayner and his teammates, coupled with my adopted dad's experience, I spent most of my time practicing in that utility room, shooting pucks at an old hockey net until the day the puck hit and broke a copper water pipe. Fortunately, the utility room was designed in case of a water issue, probably not from a puck. The gig was up.

Faith had absolutely no use for hockey or any other forms of sports, regarding people associated with these activities as lower-class, somehow inferior people. With Faith ruling the roost, it left no doubt there remained a sorry price for my adopted dad to pay for this misdeed.

Wayne was instrumental in directing me to focus primarily on my strength, endurance, and speed. Still, he stressed that all of these were subject to improving stamina, enabling you to push longer and harder during endurance exercise, lifting weights powerfully during strength training, and helping you skate faster without tiring.

I followed my workout schedule as much as possible, almost religiously. Whether running in loose, white, sandy beach soil or up and down the stadium stairs, I'd incorporate any form of building stamina I could research into the program.

I was laser-focused during the first day of the opening of tryouts at the Morishburg Pirates invitational training camp. The first day did not go as well as planned or hoped for; my nerves won the day. That night, Wayne came to visit and talked me through my anxiety, bolstering my lack of confidence and self-esteem.

With each passing day, I gained more confidence and experience that let me put everything, but the present moment out of the way. All of the training stamina I acquired was now being revealed and recognized by the coaching staff. I was called into the Coaching Staff Office on the final day of tryouts. I was welcomed to the Pirates organization and told

I'd meet with a Top Draft Hockey Agent before signing with the Morishburg Pirates.

Donnie Brooke was ecstatic, and Teddy was happy for me. We had yet to mention this to Faith, as it could rekindle issues for Donnie. I only played three-quarters of that first season when the sidewalk tragedy struck, ending any chances for a hockey career as a professional hockey player.

Even though my career as a hockey player was cut short, I still got to experience the thrill of hearing the crowd roar, the ups and downs of the game, and the strong bond between teammates and coaches. This amazing experience convinced me to pursue a new career path as a hockey coach.

This brings me to today. As I entered the arena, I acknowledged that each day's session identified a wider gap between those who could make the cut in the junior leagues and those who had reached their abilities level at junior. While discussing these matters with my assistant coach and having a beer at our local pub, Jeff again suggested I get a life outside of hockey.

"Seriously, what else do you have except hockey?"

Jeff knew about my upbringing with my grandparents and journeying with my grandfather, which seemed to matter to me. One of his friends joined a group that aimed to better understand the most widely practiced shamanic journey techniques across many different cultures.

This practice involves a form of meditation that utilizes visualization and is accompanied by repetitive and rhythmic drumming. These people met at the Culture Center once a month with shamanic leaders and Elders who eagerly shared their experiences. He suggested this activity might be an ideal place to reconnect with life outside of hockey, the right time to bond again with this facet of my past.

# Conflicting Priorities

As I walked to the arena the next day, I couldn't help but reflect on my conversation with Jeff at the pub the night before. We had a lengthy discussion about who had the potential to make the cut and who would likely not. But what stuck with me was when he pointed out my lack of social life.

The bitter Nor'Easter from the Northwest Territories made the walk to the arena cold. Growing up in this environment made harsh weather more commonplace, not any easier to deal with, just more commonplace.

My mind returned to my younger days, those I shared with my two best friends back in Witchenbrook. Little Buck and Vince were closer to being my brother than Teddy ever felt during this period of our youth. Like me, Little Buck's mom was also a native of Osaken, and his dad was also a non-native. Vince's parents were of European descent and lived near my grandparents' home on the outskirts of Witchenbrook.

The long rope bridge that spanned the Osaken River was one of our favorite places, and we'd race across this on our way to go fishing at our secret fishing pool. Little Buck's dad taught us how to spearfish using a bow and clean them. Existing seemed calm and peaceful back then, with life as gentle as the flow of the Osaken River.

As I entered the arena and headed for my office, my mind returned to the social area of my life. How often have I been in a decent and promising relationship that always ended in disaster because I was not committed to developing it further, to the next level, always putting the relationship second to my hockey career?

As I was passing Jeff's office, he called out to me.

"Hey, Anthony, this might sound reminiscent. Billy Armstrong called this morning. He fell on an icy sidewalk and went to the hospital for X-rays of his knee. I mentioned to Kenny that Billy would be calling in later."

This incident brought back a memory, alright, a harrowing one. Hearing these words reminded me that Kenny was a good trainer, one of the best; if anyone could rehabilitate your damaged knee, Kenny would be my choice. He was my choice. In my case, the damage exceeded anyone's rehabilitation limit.

One moment, your life is being laid out before you. For years, you have kept everything as much as possible focused on that one main objective, in my case, to become a professional Hockey Player in the NHL, and all the hours dedicated to intensive and systematic training returned dividends in all the areas required in this ever-increasing demand for speed and endurance in hockey at the NHL professional level.

How often I relive those last moments when all of this was still feasible and easily within reason. Everything indicated that the door to my professional future was soon to open, with my agent receiving strong interest from many NHL teams' scouts.

Then, in an instant, this damaged sidewalk, now filled with black ice, had stripped that possibility from my future. This incident seemed to happen in slow motion, with the joint tendons being torn away from the muscle. The aspiration of my lifetime was to get to this moment, now taking only a moment to terminate my career.

Sitting at my desk, trying to plan my day, I couldn't help, but think about my nonexistent social life. At the same time, I realized that my brother Teddy also needed to make time for a long-term relationship. As circumstances dictated, Teddy was always in his hospital with the current shortage of medical personnel and too many patients; with Teddy being a recognized surgeon, his celebrated operating skills were constantly in demand.

Admitting there is a trade-off for everything in life, we are trading off doing something different for everything we do. The trade-off of our respective occupations left us little to no time to visit with our Grandfather WiKenja, never mind anything resembling a developing intimate relationship.

Thinking about my trade-off today, finding myself in a blustery winter snowstorm in a concrete city, inside a cold arena, meant I couldn't be lying on a warm sunny beach down south on an exotic island as I threw a dart at the Tropical Paradise Island poster on my office wall.

Note to self: Sometimes, Anthony, you overthink and diminish what you do have at hand.

There is an inevitable adrenaline rush whenever a hockey player steps onto the ice to the crowd's roar. I truly relished the opportunity when it presented itself, one where a freak knee injury would suddenly end my playing career. I joined Jeff and Kenny on the ice as the boys were skating, warming up, and getting ready for the morning workout. Kenny said that Billy's X-rays showed no serious issues, and Billy should be back skating sometime next week.

Good news has been a rare commodity lately for the Morishburg Pirates after last year's miserable playoff series, attested by our ousting in four straight games. Thankfully, management still had confidence that their coaching staff was competent for at least one more year.

The good news continued with Kenny handing out cigars after practice. He had just become a grandfather to a beautiful baby girl. Acknowledging that Kenny could maintain a promising career and couple his career with family life gave me more hope for the right person to walk through my door one day.

We spent the remainder of the week practicing power skating and endurance development as the game increased speed with each new season. We had reduced the team's roster by three, with two more cuts needed to meet the league's regulations of signed players for the upcoming season.

I met Kenny in the local pub, and he informed Jeff and me that Billy would begin skating the following Monday. Never missing a good opportunity knowing when I'm in a good mood, Jeff suggested, "I meant to tell you, Anthony."

"You are invited to my sister Barbara's birthday party Saturday night, and she has someone she would like to introduce to you. No presents, just good wishes, and it's a BYOB."

"What is it with your family?"

"Do you get paid by a dating app to connect people?"

"Come on, Jeff, I'll be there because I think Barbara is a sweetheart, but don't push me, and don't expect me to be grateful."

"Besides, with my track record, you are doing this young woman a disservice with what you know about my dating history."

Good times, terrific music, and a party atmosphere to die for would justly describe Barbara's birthday party. Barbara's friend Jo-Anne was stunning with a personality to match, but that word always seemed to enter the equation. But there was no evident chemistry between us. We exchanged phone numbers more to appease Jeff and Barbara than to ever consider contacting each other.

On the way home from Barbara's party, contemplating this 'match-making', I remembered Miranda, what a remarkable woman she was, and how I unintentionally severely hurt her as we were one step from becoming engaged.

My inner voice alerted me that this was not the right woman for me. I warned my inner voice that it had better be right about this one because Miranda had everything I was looking for, or at least I thought she had.

It's difficult to avoid thinking about the past and wondering what could have been. I hope that someday I'll meet someone who truly connects with me and confirms that I made the right decision by following my instincts, even if it was a costly mistake. For now, it's just wishful thinking.

I went to visit my Grandfather WiKenja on Sunday. It was a long drive up to Witchenbrook. Still, the fall colors quietly consumed the time. They let me enter a peaceful mindset that had been sorely missing since early September.

I was behind the wheel of my old but trusted friend, my Willys Jeep, and we were out on the open road again, experiencing the fresh, crisp countryside air. My spirit was released, accessible, and wandering with pure abandonment.

While nearing Witchenbrook, watching for the exit for Highway 14, my old, near adolescent stomping grounds. Halfway along Highway 14, I slowed down a little more while passing by 'Dusty's Restaurant', once the only place to be on a hot summer's day, now all boarded up and abandoned.

I still remember when Grandmother Dawnlilly would bring Teddy and me to get one of their famous milkshakes, where you would get at least a glass and a half from one of those stainless steel mixing beakers.

I noticed that many of the old homes my friends grew up in were either pretty worn down or in complete disrepair. Sadly, many others no longer existed, only now being ghostly images in my mind.

There used to be an old dirt sand road illegally connected to the highway, but even then, it was easy enough to miss if you weren't watching for it. It never did have a road sign, let alone an official name. Locally, everyone knew it as 'Fishing Bridge Road'. Slowing down even more, I didn't want to miss exploring this old road and the memories it possessed for me.

This old sand road led to the 'fishing bridge' where my grandfather and I often spent time fishing. We usually talked more than fishing, which suited me as I had no inherited fishing skills. This road sure had seen better days, as this detour was a challenge even in my Jeep.

When I arrived at the old bridge, it became apparent that even my trustworthy old Jeep would not be crossing this dilapidated old bridge. While nearing the bridge, my memory vividly detailed this old bridge and the experiences shared.

Looking at this old bridge today, I witnessed the results of nature's conquest when maintenance ceases. Over the decades, the Oasken

River's constant presence had slowly converted the past into the present again, with these erosive results leaving me no option, but to backtrack when I returned to the highway after having a word with this old friend.

I got out and gingerly walked on what remained of the old fishing bridge. Nothing appeared stable as the freshwater passed under and around my old wooden friend, consuming all but what remained visible.

I sat on the riverbank for a few more minutes, remembering some of the more comical ways we landed fish. In most cases, they outsmarted us, and the last we saw of them was when they were flopping their way back along the river's bank to the safety of the water. It's too bad that Teddy never had any interest in fishing.

Life as I knew it stood perfectly still at this moment, a brief, extraordinary moment—still enough for me to enjoy these images from my past for a few more precious seconds. How do events at the moment often have so much more value than when recalled in a memory?

This is often the time in my life when a lesson is learned, but if there is a lesson here, I don't see it.

Driving my old Jeep back to the highway, I thought of one of my two best friends, Vince, who rebuilt this old World War II vintage Willys Jeep from junk and spare parts he found. This old Jeep is just as stubborn as Vince and continues to be of service many years later. Vince spent his youth buying and rebuilding dilapidated, abandoned relics of old trucks or World War II vintage jeeps, bringing them back to life for one more go-around, finding his life niche.

As I continued driving along Highway 14, enjoying the memories certain sights and places provoked, they brought an awareness of how our youth and lifetime seem infinite. The reality is quite different, and all things considered, maybe that's a good thing.

Turning into my grandfather's long, winding driveway also triggered many forgotten memories. I noticed the trees had grown taller while still trying to avoid washouts, and the driveway soon needed tender loving care.

Oh, the memories of tobogganing down the driveway in the winter chasing Teddy, with Grandmother Dawnlilly cheering us on. I can still see her rosy cheeks telling us she'd make her famous hot cocoa and an ice cream float for us when we went back up to the warm house that was always waiting for us. Today, the driveway seemed much shorter and decidedly less steep than those many bygone yesterdays.

The house, too, looked a little older and needed some obvious maintenance in the not-too-distant future. I couldn't help but notice that after all of these many years, the old screen door was still missing its center hinge.

During the hot, humid mid-summer nights, when all the windows and doors were left open, the only hope was that the day's heat would surrender to the cool night air, cooling off the house so we could sleep; for this reason, often with the front door left open in the summer. I would face this old screen door from my bed, looking past my bedroom door to the screen door, letting my imagination escape into the unknown.

Hoping the screen door wouldn't fall off in my hand; I opened the main door entrance and walked into the house. Then I heard the voice I so dearly longed to hear.

"Kenja, Kenja, Kenja, how I've missed you, son, how I've missed you."

# The Breakthrough

Attempting to become a professional hockey player consumed every other aspect of my young life. I spent every moment in an arena, gym training, or any other venue while building muscle strength, stamina, and endurance.

Upon entering the Culture Center, I realized how highly isolated my existence had become. Apart from my male friends, who were usually connected to hockey, I had no social life and had lost the desire to engage with society.

Opening the door and walking into the center, I was greeted by an atmosphere that had long been missing recently. This aura of togetherness, and welcomeness, returned me to the time I lived with my grandparents and what a heartwarming existence it had provided for me in my young life.

While entering the door, I noticed the handcrafted wooden handles were similar to those in and around Witchenbrook, making the experience almost familiar. The people assembled here today were wide in age and nationality. Noting at least a 50/50 split in gender was also an abnormality for me, a very nice one.

I continued going to the Culture Center once a month while slowly acknowledging my desire and need to communicate and socialize with various people participating. I felt even more like a fish out of the water while attempting to build confidence in engaging with women, and there was one, in particular, I found very attractive.

Not only was Celeste stunning and intelligent, but she also had a quirky sense of humor. She was so outgoing and friendly. But acknowledging my hidden shyness was now so apparent as I got deeper into these foreign, uncharted waters.

I had planned my opening pick-up line for the first three meetings with Celeste, but things don't always go as planned. As I stood there, lost in thought about how to approach her, I felt a tap on my shoulder. I turned around to see who it was.

"Hi, I'm Celeste. How are you?"

As I found myself unexpectedly in front of Celeste, I could only imagine how my facial expression must have appeared. I repeatedly reminded myself to stay calm, think twice before speaking, or more likely stammering, and not ruin this opportunity before it even began.

I physically sensed my Grandmother Dawnlilly squeezing my hand and filling my heart with warmth, reminding me that the longest journey starts with a single step, and this step might be your new beginning.

After the meeting, Celeste and I went to a nearby cafe and talked for what seemed like hours, but was in reality, minutes. Before going our separate ways, we revealed some parts of our backgrounds. Okay, I did a lot of nodding, but it was the right thing to do as we exchanged phone numbers at the end of the talk and set up our next getting-together for coffee.

With our friendship growing, we began meeting outside the Culture Center. In doing so, I was introduced to new people while associating with more of Celeste's friends, of whom there were many.

To say I was enthralled and captive to her charm would easily trivialize matters; witnessing her passion for life and the contentment she found was enticing.

I still recall when my Grandmother Dawnlilly talked to me about finding my soulmate. She mentioned a unique feeling, like beautiful monarch butterflies fluttering in your stomach, deep within that is hard to describe yet impossible to ignore.

I don't remember ever being so optimistic about what life had to offer while simultaneously being so nervous about how easily something like this emotion could shatter like a crystal.

These were similar words that my Grandmother Dawnlilly had spoken to me when I sought to find out how my mom and dad first met. She described this bubbly enthusiasm, wanting to tell everyone in sight, one of those, 'What, you can't see this' moments. She was still trying not to be too obvious, but honestly, it is impossible to hide such a feeling of awareness.

The twinkle in Celeste's eyes, her beaming smile, and the way she'd jump into my arms unexpectedly and squeeze me with an indescribable passion dispensed with any notion of any soulmate mismatch. She had a very teasing nature, one she delighted in repeatedly catching me off-guard with.

We continued to journey with the elders and shamans at the Culture Center once a month. As we shared these experiences with our newfound friends at the center, they quickly became like family to us. For once, I felt I had finally gotten off the 'Train of Life' at the right station this time.

Captivating would best describe my last journeying experience, a spellbinding adventure. Upon my return to this parallel world, I found it challenging to convey the insights I had gained. I became overly emotional and frustrated as I tried to communicate these insights to Celeste and others. My lack of a suitable interpretation made me sorely agitated, further compounding the problem.

It took a long time to commit to returning from my previous journey, with unimaginable conflicts trying to prevent me from doing so. The temptation to ignore the drumming dictating the necessity of returning from this land of untold mysteries was so powerful and draining. I've often felt extreme exhaustion when I returned home, but nothing quite like this.

Celeste and I became inseparable as our relationship blossomed and extended into every facet of our hopes and dreams, ones we wanted to share. Celeste also became interested in hockey and was now attending many of our home games. I constantly heard Grandmother Dawnlilly telling me not to become possessive and mess this one up, or, as

Grandfather said in simple language, a control freak, take heed of that little voice inside of you.

Celeste and one of her best friends, Vienna, were committed to and involved with a Save the Children Campaign program, becoming executive members and constantly fundraising.

One afternoon, I was at home in my apartment trying to unload nagging issues using my journeying rattle and drum without any particular intention, only to escape from my daily routine, starting with a steady beat. Gradually, I found myself saying these words along with the drumming. I jotted them down and wondered if they could be helpful in Celeste's and Vienna's future promotional fundraising efforts.

*The Fairies danced*
*And the Minstrels played.*
*Turning Night Time into Day*
*And the drumming grew.*
*As the Flames did too*
*So did the Path*
*that the Lost Child Knew*
*Would lead to your Land of*
*Freedom*

They liked the results and felt it, in a way, conveyed their fundraising intent to their donors in giving the hope of freedom to these lost children. I certainly didn't have the money, not the kind they needed, so having them accept my verse was one way for me to contribute.

Meeting with our friends at the Culture Center as often as life permitted, Celeste and I looked forward to our next chance to journey and, in my case, hoping to relive that one unique journey I continued to treasure.

Things go alright on some hockey road trips; others are best forgotten. During this road trip, the Morishburg Pirates hadn't done much pirating for the better part of the last two weeks, losing three out of the four away games. The officiating sucked during the entire trip, but during this final game, it was so blatantly obvious these refs were homers, and I was so upset that I finally lost all control.

Jeff tried to intervene and calm me down enough to regain my composure, telling me we would be in 'heart attack' territory if I let my emotions continually become dominant. With the Ref finally ejecting me from the game, Kenny took me to our dressing room as I continued chirping.

After returning home, I was physically nearing disproportionate exhaustion and mentally needed to take a break from hockey and the arena for a few days. Tonight, there was a scheduled meeting at the Culture Center. Jeff and Kenny will handle the morning practice and tell the players I got my 'Rabies Shot' and should be fine in a day or two.

At every opportunity, I continued to attempt to access that one fantastic journey again, experiencing the encompassing land of untold beauty and experiences that seemed impossible. It is one of those cases where trying too hard is the culprit.

As usual, all our newfound friends had gathered at the Cultural Center as we exchanged greetings and waited as our Shaman lit sage and sweet grass in preparation for this evening's journeying experience, filling the air with smoke for smudging. The accompanying drums and rattles brought the tranquility I sorely needed.

I felt exhausted while talking to Doug about the bowl he had made taking his woodturning lessons and the amazing Patina he managed to achieve. Celeste took my hand as we prepared to be seated; I mentioned I wasn't feeling myself at all tonight. I clearly needed to relax and escape hockey and its demanding daily life.

# No Way Home

The start of this experience was very different from anything I had previously encountered. I can't recall entering any porthole or hearing the drumming beat escorting me to my entry. Yet, here I was, overwhelmed with colors that were so vivid, so foreign to anything remotely seen on Earth or any other journeying experiences. The countless numbers of creatures materialized in unbounded beauty everywhere I looked. I was caught between the proverbial 'rock and a hard place' as I journeyed through this alluring mystical network of endless wonders.

The obsession to continue my journey had manifested into an uncontrollable urge to ignore shamanic teachings and sacrifice everything to continue to exist here for just a few more precious moments. There was an unfamiliar sense of anxiety this time.

I never heard the drumming either, indicating the need to return. Still, I had never encountered anything as spellbinding as this enchanting music dancing in my soul. Something strange was a flutter, affecting my heart at this very moment.

As I turned to leave, the enchanting music overwhelmed my very being and continued to surround me mystically. Looking back, I tried to recall the drumming or even if the porthole's closure had existed. Something was different this time, but I wasn't sure what.

Anxiously, I scoured the landscape where I hoped to find the porthole. In a panic, I realized I had broken the most sacred guiding principle by entering without my power animal, the red-tailed hawk, but even more so by not returning when the drum beat quickened; I didn't hear the sounding drum beat to return. Whatever, I have seemingly forfeited the one opportunity to return home. How can I be so stupid?

Now seemingly orphaned once again in this parallel world.

A voice from within the music, "What is your name?"

Startled, I turned around, "What, where did you come from?"

"I came along the rock pathway that leads from every to where."

Looking me up and down, "Don't you have a name?"

"Kenja."

"Strange name; where are you from, Kenja?"

"Earth."

"Is Earth far from here?"

"I don't know. Where are we?"

"We're here, you silly Kenja from Earth."

"What is your name?"

"You can call me Celeste."

"Is that your name?"

"No, but it's a good name, don't you think?"

"My name is Pati'na."

"I think Patina is a good name, Celeste."

"Not Patina; it's Pati'na."

"Well, you appear to have a beautiful patina for such a young girl, Pati'na. What is the name of this place, Pati'na?"

"You are on Modeerf, Kenja from Earth."

"Please, can you call me just Kenja?"

We sat and continued talking while resting at the bank of a gently flowing stream: the lighting made its ripples sparkle and dance. I asked Pati'na what the name of her village was and how far it might be.

According to Pati'na, their village, Ecaps, had a fixed location. Still, it was always nearby as it started everywhere and ended anywhere while traveling with you. Whenever you feel exhausted or seek guidance, you can sit down, focus on visualizing Ecaps, and ask the Fate-Keepers to enter your life, providing direction and advice.

"How long are the daylight hours here, Pati'na?"

Pati'na told me they could be as long or as short as the thoughts in a moment. Our conversation exposed me to a new logic and reasoning in Modeerf.

Pati'na: "Come, Just Kenja. Let me take you to our village and introduce you to my Fate-Keepers and parents. I will be your Cicerone during your familiarization here on Modeerf."

"My Cicerone, I know that word. It's an ancient word."

Pati'na: "This is an ancient place."

'Just Kenja, eh!' I realized I would have to be more careful with my wording here on Modeerf. I'll have to tell my grandfather that my first lesson learned on this journey was 'that words matter'.

We traveled along a trail that was neither suspended nor connected to anything. Yet the vegetation seemed to react to the weight of our movement. My Grandfather WiKenja will be interested in these lessons learned if I can one day return home. As I witnessed all these new ideas unfolding before me, it felt like the Earth was a far-off memory.

I never noticed the trail transforming into a cobblestone rocky pathway, as slowly, the village emerged behind the waterfall, where the stream ended. This gentle glen encompassed picturesque houses and shops dotting the landscape.

"This place is Ecaps, our home village and beacon."

Her stunning smile flashed as Pati'na reached out for a well-weathered hand that was greeting her, introducing me, "This is my father, Sawenco. This is Just Kenja."

Sawenco then motioned to his wife, Yadretsey, to come and meet Just Kenja. Yadretsey, too, seemed a somewhat fragile woman. She seemed elderly to have such a young daughter in Pati'na, who said they call her mom Yada for short. At least, Yada is one name I will have a chance to remember.

We arrived just as Pati'na's parents were about to eat. They asked if I would like to join them for this meal; I was hungry and hadn't noticed the time of day. I didn't know if there was a time of day here on Modeerf.

As the day's activities came to a close, my thoughts returned to the offset of this journey I embarked on while lying beside Celeste, one with the sole intention of returning to this place I had once experienced, one that had cultivated this maddening desire to return, to the point of becoming an addiction.

*What was this all about when Pati'na first introduced herself as Celeste? It raised questions; her casual and convincing demeanor suggested it to be more than a coincidence. What is the connection? Is there a connection?*

I noticed that Pati'na had finished helping her mother, Yada, with the after-dinner chores. She was now heading in my direction with that happy-go-lucky assurance of a young woman who knew precisely her lot in life.

"I'm glad you have met my family, Just Kenja."

"They were pleased to have met you and your calming nature."

My 'calming nature', is not a phrase usually associated with any description of my character, at least recently.

"Your parents seem very proud of you and your achievements, Pati'na."

"It is obvious that you have a very close-knit family."

"I don't know what 'close-knit 'means, but it sounds positive with this combination of these two familiar words, Just Kenja."

"Do you have a family back on your Earth?"

"I do, Pati'na. It is not a very large one, though."

"I have an older brother, Teddy, and my grandfather, WiKenja, who raised Teddy and me when we were orphaned with the death of our parents when we were still infants."

"I'm sorry to learn of this tragedy, Just Kenja, but also pleased to learn that you and your brother remained connected to the family through your adoption."

"Well, we weren't adopted by our grandparents, more to the fact that the courts awarded us to their custody, Pati'na."

"The most important thing to me, Just Kenja, is that you and Teddy remain part of your family. Our family in Ecaps on Modeerf gives our life true meaning. Is it similar on your Earth?"

"It was for my grandparents and me."

"Pati'na. I think being a family member was for Teddy too, but he had a lot of difficulty expressing emotions of any sort; I would suspect that we mean as much to him as he does to us."

"I remember when my Grandfather WiKenja gave me some wood and taught me how to carve it, Pati'na."

"I carved a sign about being in a family, and my Grandmother Dawnlilly proudly hung it in the entranceway to their home near their main door, where I think it continues to hang today."

"Wow, I would like to know what words were so meaningful that you carved them into a piece of wood. Do you remember what you wrote, Just Kenja?"

"Oh ya, for sure, Pati'na,

### Family

A Family is never to be alone
Even when you are by yourself.
And being able to be yourself
Not only when you are alone"

"Thanks for sharing this, Just Kenja. I find it telling."

I heard her singing to herself as she walked away;

"My new friend, Just Kenja from Earth, even though he's not at home, he's not alone here."

With Pati'na returning to her family, I switched my thoughts to finding a means of soon returning to Earth and my family, including Celeste. At least, in my mind, Celeste was a part of it; I intended to ask her to marry me when I returned home.

How did I mess up this decision to ignore the drumming, dictating my return and creating my third mistake? I'm still not 100% sure I ever heard the drumming, for that matter. What was that all about? My grandfather said that only the most determined would make the same mistake a third time. He will be genuinely disappointed with my apparent lack of judgment, never mind my misplaced concern about Celeste's worry, which I have no doubt created.

# The Near Tragedy

Awoken with someone tapping me on my feet, finding myself snuggly wrapped in a cocoon hammock, I slowly open my eyes. I've never been someone who can act upon waking; I've always struggled.

"Good morning, Just Kenja."

"I wasn't sure if I should wake you as you were deep asleep."

"Hey, Pati'na."

"No, it's fine that you woke me."

We walked back to Pati'na's parents' home. It was a warm morning if it was morning. I did not notice any sunset last night or sunrise here on Modeerf. Maybe today, some answers still need to be revealed.

"My parents had a meeting to go to this morning, Just Kenja, but they asked me again to tell you they enjoyed meeting you."

"Yes, it was nice meeting them too, Pati'na."

"So, it wasn't nice meeting me?"

"What? No, that's not what I meant."

I think my inexperience around women has raised its ugly head again. Finding myself stammering while searching for the words before I dig myself deeper.

"You're just too easy to tease, Just Kenja."

"And apparently, you, Pati'na, are just the right person to ensure it happens."

"And by the way, the jury is still out with the decision on meeting you, Pati'na."

"I don't know what a jury is, Just Kenja, but I'm sure they'll make the right decision."

So the day began. My mind was torn between finding my way home as soon as possible and opting to experience what was apparently available. If only I had my red-tailed hawk here for protection.

"Your parents seem so happy together. Did they meet here in Ecaps at a young age, or was it later in life?"

"Your question would need lots of answers, Just Kenja."

"I didn't mean to pry, but after a seemingly long marriage, it's nice to see how much they still care for each other as often these days on Earth, longevity in a marriage is often not the case. Pati'na."

"Well, their marriage was odd in its day, Just Kenja."

"Really, would they mind if you told me more, Pati'na?"

"No, I'm sure they would be alright with this. Actually, they are kind of proud of how things turned out."

"When they were both young, Ecaps and Unknowns were distant communities that lived in harmony with all of the other surrounding communities. My father's family was from Ecaps, and my mother's was from Unknowns."

"Was this a problem, Pati'na?"

"Not until they fell in love, Just Kenja."

"At that time, most, if not everyone, married someone within their community as the population was large and travel was limited."

"My mother, Yadretsey, and her sister, Itsey, were part of a group of young Unknowns that were out foraging with some elders."

"There is only one known predator to the people of Modeerf, and that's the flesh-eating Klongs that can be found throughout Modeerf."

"So, these Klongs, are they large or small in size?"

"They are big and agile, and they are cunning and fast, Just Kenja."

"Are they here around Ecaps?"

"They prefer less open areas, wooded or thick dense vegetation to hunt their prey. But, yes, at times, they can be found anywhere."

"So, what happened to have your parents meet?"

"While Yada and Itsey were out foraging with the others, they became surrounded by some Klongs. The elders headed the young into an open area while they prepared to defend and needed to slay the Klongs quickly."

"Itsey and Yada never made it to the clearing. Itsey tripped, breaking her leg, and Yada pulled her into a small gully, gathering brush to cover them."

"Before the terrifying onslaught ended, the savagery of this group of Klongs was ferocious, enough to make someone's blood run cold while witnessing two young people being dragged away and killed by the Klongs.

"The elders had surrounded the young people, having them dig into the dry sandy soil, making mounds of sand. Each time the Klongs attacked, they tried to repel them by throwing sand and dust in their eyes. After a long, deadly, gruesome battle, two of these outnumbered and horrified elders had succumbed to their wounds; it was also assumed that the Klongs must have ravished both Yada and Itsey before they could make their way to the clearing with the others."

"It was just by chance that my father, Sawenco, was fishing with a group of boys from Ecaps around this same time. Apparently, my father was not too adept at orienting in the wilderness, and he, too, got separated from his group."

"This sounds like the making of a good movie, Pati'na."

"I'm sorry, Just Kenja, I don't know what a movie is."

When will I ever learn not to needlessly interrupt? Apparently, not today.

"My father knew to follow any waterway downstream, often leading to a village and safety. While making camp for the night, he heard some rustling; too noisy to be Klongs, so he investigated, finding my mother and her sister."

"Yada had set Itsey's leg the best she could, keeping them both alive. My father built a better shelter and prepared some foods with constant fire burning, keeping them warm and dry while keeping the Klongs away. Two things happened as a result of these hostilities, Just Kenja. This unnatural, aggressive action by the Klongs attacking in such an open area was very uncharacteristic of them, and the Unknown leaders decided that it was best to relocate further away from this area and build a fortified compound for their community. All hope of ever finding Yada or Itsey during this period was exhausted."

"What was the second thing to happen, Pati'na?"

"The Ecaps Chief of Council assembled their best trackers and some volunteers at the Assembly Hall and devised a plan to search and recover young Sawecno. Once they found the stream, they knew with Sawenco's recent orientation and survival training this was the probable route he would have followed. It wasn't long before the search and rescue party was returning with all three of the survivors back to Ecaps."

"It must have been harrowing for them trying to survive, Pati'na. I can only imagine how Yada and Sawecno struggled to prevent Itsey from getting seriously infected."

"Once Yada and Itsey had time to recover and adjust to life in Ecaps, they were welcomed by the couple who raised them as their own, now becoming a member of the Ecaps community."

"So, this is how your parents met. Did their love story start soon afterward?"

"Not really, Just Kenja. Itsey, Yada, my father, his best friend Olund, and some of their close friends started hanging out together. But there always was this obvious connection between Yada and Sawecno that eventually blossomed into their marriage."

"It sounds like it was meant to be and would be regardless of the obstacles placed in their way, Pati'na."

"Although Itsey and Yada were accepted in Ecaps, marriage to a person from outside of Ecaps was not so easily accepted, and for reasons I don't know, more so for any one of the Unknowns. My father's parents welcomed Yada and were pleased to learn of their son Sawecno's intent to ask Yada to become his wife. Olund's parents supported their son's desire to marry Itsey, even though she wasn't from their community."

"It wasn't always easy for them to fit in, be accepted. Yada and Itsey influenced the community positively, gaining acceptance as community members of Ecaps."

"Shortly after my parents were married, Itsey and my father's best friend Olund were also married, with both couples making every effort to create a home and eventually a family in Ecaps as their friendship continued to grow."

"So, can I assume that your mother gave birth to you soon afterward?"

"No, not early in their marriage, Just Kenja. They waited until they were confident they would make a suitable presentation and impression on the grandmothers when the time came."

I heard the words all right, but they didn't make any sense to me. Obviously, they did spark my curiosity.

"This story has already been very intriguing, but why do I feel the best is yet to come, Pati'na? What would their grandmothers have to do with them starting a family? I don't understand."

"Not their grandmothers, Just Kenja, the Grandmothers of Ecaps."

"That doesn't help much yet. I'm guessing I'm missing the important pieces in all of this, Pati'na. Though I am more than curious to understand what you are telling me."

"On Modeerf and in this case in particular, in Ecaps, when people want to start having children to start a family, they must make their presentation before the Grandmothers of Ecaps. These women have the authority to decide who does or does not merit this privilege of parenthood. There is no male input in the narrative or composition of the process and only female 'elders' can become a member of the Grandmothers."

"This is so much more than simply interesting, Pati'na."

The image of my grandmother is the brightest I have ever seen. Even my grandfather will be intrigued by what might be revealed soon.

"On Earth, all females capable of conceiving are able to either naturally by conception or by artificial fertilization, with the female carrying the fetus in her womb for about nine months. Is it similar here on Modeerf, Pati'na?"

"On Earth, the baby actually develops inside the mother, Just Kenja?"

"Of course, that's how pregnancy and the birth of a child always happen, Pati'na."

"On Modeerf, the child is created in the water of nature's womb and welcomed by the parents when the creation has been completed, Just Kenja."

Hearing these words describe the birthing process here on Modeerf, and it was a creation, not a birth. Perhaps governing who can and can not rear children has a degree of merit. Regardless, the loss of connection between the mother and child is unimaginable for me to understand.

Even at eighteen months of age, I registered an unknown connection with my mother, and this loss took a severe toll on my development. One thing that struck me now is how the interaction with Pati'na and her parents mimicked more of the connection I have with my grandparents. But not the motherly love I witnessed between Mother Mary and Vince.

Once again, 'It has been said that you can't miss something that has never been experienced or you are unaware of'. What a valuable lesson I've learned today, Grandfather. Whether human or from the animal kingdom, this motherly connection is something to behold; witnessing a birth brings out the mother in first-time mothers.

"I'm getting hungry, Just Kenja. How about you? Are you hungry yet?"

"This would be a good time to eat and for me to digest a few things, Pati'na."

# Finding Little People

"How was lunch, Just Kenja?"

"It was great, and I was surprised how so little food could fill me up, but it sure did."

"So, what are these vegetables, and are they unique vegetables grown here on Modeerf?"

"It's more the way they are watered at the Tangled Garden, Just Kenja."

I'm sensing that visiting the Tangled Garden is on the agenda, if not today, on the agenda nonetheless.

"That sounds interesting, Pati'na."

Man, how can you possibly sound so drab? You are such a klutz around women, even here on Modeerf.

"I would like to revisit that waterway we walked beside on our way to Ecaps. I found it fascinating and would like to explore it again, Pati'na."

"It's one of my favorite places here on Modeerf, too, Just Kenja."

"I'm glad you like it too."

"I'll tell my parents before we go."

Once more, we walked along with captivating sights abounding everywhere as we returned to the trail where the free-floating exotic flowers abounded; this stunning vegetation seemed to welcome us as it seemingly danced to our movements. Coming to a fork in the path, I realized that we were now heading into a new area of Modeerf, one I eagerly waited to explore with Pati'na.

This peaceful trail was now converting to a smaller path alongside a fast-flowing and meandering waterway, considerably broader and faster than the one we had already experienced yesterday.

"You picked a good time to visit Modeerf, Just Kenja."

"My friend Yerlaw told me he was here earlier and noticed that the Cuffer's annual spawning run had already started, and although the run is only beginning, it looked like it would be a good year for the Cuffer's migration."

"And even having witnessed this ritual often, he said they were pretty awe-inspiring even for him, so I'm hoping you find them enticing too, Just Kenja."

"What is inspiring, and who is Yerlaw, Pati'na?"

"Like I said, Just Kenja, the Cuffers are inspiring; you just wait and see."

"And Yerlaw is a good and longtime friend I'm sure you'll likely meet."

"So, you have salmon here on Modeerf, Pati'na?"

"I don't know what a salmon is, but when you see the Cuffers, they might be the same. You tell me."

"We should crossover here, Just Kenja. The stream widens even more around the next bend where the flow also gets considerably quicker, dividing in two with the one soon turning into rapids, leading to a sizable waterfall."

I can't wait to see this more rapidly flowing water, or maybe I should wait because if these aren't rapids, I may not want to see them then. The flow here is wickedly fast, never mind seeing this much water cascading over a waterfall.

"Do you want me to go first, or would you like to crossover first, Just Kenja?"

"Well, Pati'na, I don't see a bridge anywhere."

"How do you propose we get across? These waters aren't a babbling brook, are they?"

"Why would we need a bridge, Just Kenja, when we can walk across?"

*Looking at these rapids, I fear this will fail to end well. Actually, I know it won't end well. I remember when my grandfather guided me on my first journey, where I encountered these three frogs. I stopped to enjoy their music. They were all dressed in tuxedoes, standing on a Lilly pad playing jazz. That time, I scrambled across the water from Lilly pad to Lilly pad until I reached them. And I don't see any Lilly pads or anything else resembling something to get safely to the other side. I don't even see any frogs.*

"Perhaps I will follow you, Pati'na."

*Watching Pati'na walk nonchalantly, casually continuing after the trail ended, meeting the water's edge, she continued walking across the impending obstacle these rapids provided as I would walk across the Fishing Bridge back in Witchenbrook. Scratching my head, I continued watching till she reached the other side.*

"Okay, what are you waiting for, Just Kenja?"

*Yeah, what are you waiting for, Just Kenja? What seems to be your issue?*
*Well, other than drowning, there's nothing worth pointing out.*

"I'm thinking about it, Pati'na."
"Just Kenja, thinking will only provide a barrier for you to deal with."
Pati'na is now beginning to sound like my Grandmother Dawnlilly when she told me, "When you come to an obstacle, Kenja, you just have to avoid the obstacle." Oh, it should be that easy. I only wish that I could do that right now. Or, in this case, 'don't think, paint'.

"So, what you are saying, Pati'na, is that it is only mind over matter; conquer that, and then I can cross safely."

"I don't know what 'matter' means, Just Kenja."

Does it even matter here on Modeerf?

Having faith and trust in Pati'na's assured outcome is the big question. So, with a leap of blind faith, one with my eyes wide open, I visualized myself stepping onto the top of these rapids while remaining supported by who knows what and then landing on dry land.

Intent is one thing; Sometimes, success is quite another.

"That's good, Just Kenja. Let's walk until we reach the spawning river, where, hopefully, we might see some Cuffers migrating."

Reaching the other side of the riverbank while following Pati'na, I constantly looked back, trying to understand what had just happened. Eventually, we decided to sit and wait patiently to see if the Cuffers would cooperate. I felt unwell and tired again, so taking a break was a good option.

"Just Kenja, while we wait, can you tell me a little about your Earth?"

Before responding, I looked around this area, which was utterly mind-bogglingly beautiful; astonishing glimpses abound everywhere. At their free will, animals seemingly appear and disappear from their camouflage, giving me a momentary glimpse but not enough time to fully register precisely what I saw before disappearing again.

It reminded me of when we were only kids, and that day, one of my friends tried to explain that his cousin could usually hide from view whenever she wanted. He explained this by saying, "I turned around, and there she was, gone."

This sums up what these images are doing with me now. I turn around, and there they are, gone.

"Okay, Pati'na, I'll tell you back home on Earth, we have some of the best rivers, lakes, and oceans and…"

"Yahoo! Here they come, Just Kenja, look, it's the Cuffers."

"Wow, look at them all, Just Kenja."

"They are so majestic and powerful, aren't they?"

These fish were giant, enormous marine species, definitely not salmon. They were at least the size of a Dolphin, but seemingly more mighty than a freight train. I stood there, gawking in complete awe.

"Let's swim among them, Just Kenja."

Now that got my attention.

Even for Modeerf, this option sounded iffy.

"Come on, Just Kenja, take a chance."

Sure, right, or we could jump directly in front of a speeding freight train and get the same probable results.

"They won't be bothered by us."

That's precisely what I am afraid of.

"They'll more than likely invite our company."

More than likely, it is not a confidence booster for me.

"Come on; you don't want to miss this opportunity; enjoy the experience, Just Kenja."

As I entered the water with more than a little apprehension, the current was intensely threatening. Still, as Pati'na said, the Cuffers seemed to like our company. Surprisingly, I was uninhibited when I realized I didn't need to resurface for air. This unique opportunity to swim among these oversized, playful Cuffers was becoming a mad experience—simply mad.

Arriving at a pool of calm waters, nearing exhaustion, I couldn't wipe the smile from my face. Even this pain in my chest was not enough to spoil the moment.

"So, what do you think, Just Kenja? Did you enjoy it?"

"Enjoy it...Holy Shit. Are you kidding me?"

"That was simply insane. It was so mad, Pati'na, so, so mad."

"Is Holy Shit a good thing, Just Kenja?"

"Holy Shit, is a great thing, an awesome thing, Pati'na, just amazing."

Once more, we rested as I looked about in appreciation of our surroundings. There is so much to take in, no time to analyze, only moments to enjoy. Grandfather will be proud to learn of this realization that some moments are for the eyes only, not for the canvas.

"Where to next, Pati'na? My Modeerfian Cicerone."

"I'd like to go along the nearby path of the Cryptic Energies. I know something odd is happening there, but I'm never sure what it is. At times, there are these unexplainable movements in the grass. Maybe you'll see something I've been missing."

"Then, Just Kenja, we'll have to return to Ecaps as I must remember to meet with Yerlaw later this evening. Does this sound like a plan?"

"Pati'na, I can't see it possibly rivaling what I just experienced while swimming with you and the Cuffers, but let's go and seize the rest of the day anyway."

While hiking up the slope toward the Cryptic Energies fields, these vivid shades of green reminded me of the greens in the pictures in my father's old photo album of Ireland. My grandfather told me about my father Daniel's eyes and how they glistened whenever he spoke of 'his' Ireland. He always said that it was no wonder Ireland is called the Emerald Isle with its unbelievably lush greens.

One day, I would like to visit these rolling green grasses that continue growing against the ancient castles' walls, still embedded in the rocky coastal areas, continually resisting time and nature.

"Wow, Pati'na. This entire area is so alluring, with a definite sense of spiritedness. I'm also sensing a strong tingling in my arms and the nape of my neck. There's some kind of energy here."

"Look, look at the hairs on my arm, Pati'na."

"Wow…Look…they are all standing!"

"Yes, this place has been so secretive, Just Kenja."

"The Cryptic Energies always seem to be here, in this area. Although I've never seen anyone's hair stand up this way."

"I always get this sense of something different happening here, Just Kenja. But that's all I ever get, which is a sense, nothing more."

"Wow, really, this is crazy, Pati'na. Look at all the little people, holy smacking crackers."

"They bloody well exist and resemble the little people my grandfather talked about. They are known as Fairies back in Ireland, the little people of Ireland."

As Kenja turned to see if Pati'na had also noticed these little creatures scurrying about in the emerald blades of grass, he heard an angry little voice.

"Why is he calling us the little people, Paddy? Why?"

"Doesn't he know who we are, the wee folk, Paddy?"

"That's right, O' Danny Boy, we are those wee folk, Paddy."

Slapping his knee with his hand, "We are the wee and mischievous little sprites. Aren't we, Paddy?"

One of the other little green-suited fellows piped up, "We are the Leprechauns of Modeerf. Aren't we, Paddy?"

Kenja knelt, gazing at a tiny face peering from behind a giant toadstool,

"Hey...you can hear me?"

Turning back to face Pati'na to see her reaction. "Look, Pati'na. They can hear me. This is crazy, Pati'na."

"Really, Just Kenja, do you think so? Who are you speaking to?"

"Seriously, you are asking me who I am speaking to? To these little guys, Pati'na, this is so cool, so neat. Come here, and you'll see them better."

"Now you're starting to be a little more than creepy, Just Kenja."

"Pati'na, I'm not trying to freak you out. Look, I'm talking to these little people."

"Hey, you o'mucker, she can't see us," said the little voice coming from the grass.

"Who can't see you, and who are you guys anyway?"

"We are Glimps, and she, that one there, beside you, is one of 'those' who can't see us."

"That's right, Paddy, that's right."

Then Paddy pointed his finger menacing at Pati'na like a lawyer would when accusing a defendant.

"She's a Denyer."

Pati'na chirped in, "You realize you are talking to the thin air right now. There's nothing there, Just Kenja, just your imagination. Are you seriously suggesting that you are talking to something other than the grass, Just Kenja?"

"And you're seriously telling me that you honestly can't see these little people, or at least hear these little guys, Pati'na."

"Not one little peek, not one peep, Just Kenja, not one."

Once more, the little Pixie chirped up.

"Hey, strange one, where are you from?"

A second little elf-like creature jumps up, slapping Paddy on the back. "That's a wonderful question, Paddy, just wonderful."

I assumed this little Pixie was talking to me. "I'm from Earth."

Then, again, the other little excited Glimpse screamed out in jubilation, "Earth, Paddy, that's wonderful. Isn't it, Paddy, isn't it wonderful?"

As his arms stretched skyward with euphoria, he continued to whoop.

"That's wonderful, isn't it, Paddy? Absolutely wonderful."

"Don't mind him and his wee little brain. He thinks everything is wonderful."

"The other day, he had a toothache and thought that was wonderful."

"What is your blind friend's name, Irish one?"

"My name is Kenja, and Pati'na's not blind."

"It's you, little people, you Glimps, that she can't see, and I'm not Irish."

"I think he's getting a tad bit irritated with ya, Paddy. Isn't he? But that's a wonderful irritation, isn't it, Paddy? Simply wonderful."

"Okay, Kenja, take your Denyer, or whatever she wants to be called, now take her by the hand, and we tiny little Glimpse will appear before her."

"He has a Pati'na, Paddy! Isn't that wonderful, Paddy? And she's right, looker, too. Isn't that truly wonderful, Paddy?"

"Just Kenja, I don't understand anything happening here."

*Right…Welcome to my World, Pati'na.*

"They want me to take you by the hand, and if you believe in their existence, they'll appear before you, letting you see and hear them, Pati'na."

"Hold my hand, Just Kenja?"

*I wish I had dreamed this up to hold her hand. I honestly do.*

I reached out, taking her hand.

Suddenly, a sheer shriek of pure ecstasy burst from Pati'na. Thrilled would be a good word.

"Look at all these little people. Just Kenja, look at them."

"How did you say it? Holy smacking crackers!"

"They call themselves Glimps, Pati'na, and they are adorable little creatures, aren't they?"

This was one of those moments when life offered a chance to pass on or connect with opportunity.

Pati'na and I were intrigued by just meeting these 'little people', these Glimps. We stayed visiting as they continually surprised us with their antics, talents, and mastery of entertainment.

They could undoubtedly quickly fill a place like Carnegie Hall with their majestic music alone. Their undeniable power to comfort any audience instantly connects their uplifting performance with an ability to entertain and inspire.

We spent the remainder of the day amused by their antics and theatrical performance, especially Paddy and the little fellow who found everything wonderful. It made me appreciate they found their special place, that wonderful sweet spot, with how and where to live. Could it be that simple?

"By acknowledging the vast power of love around you, to see the improbable."

# The Awakening

I opened my eyes, awakening in a suspended, encompassing cocoon-styled hammock, looking around to realize that my journey was a journey, not just a dream.

This place is oddly unique, so different from any place I have previously journeyed to. Unimaginable would be a fitting word to describe this adventure to my grandfather. He'll want more than one word, but it would be a good starting point. The vegetation is multi-hued shades of green everywhere I look, contrasting with an ever-changing, vivid array of foreign colors.

Laying here, captivated by my new surroundings, I quickly drifted into my subconscious, more profoundly, looking for clarity in some of my rambling thoughts.

I'm so fortunate I don't have to understand everything life occasionally throws at me. Supposing I only accept some parts, would that matter? Because there are 'parts' to be played by each of us, as many have already noted, 'aren't we all actors in this stage of life'. One where once we accept that laughter can consume tears and perhaps turn a nightmare into a dream, our scene in life's curtain lifts?

Illnesses and diseases are not terminal. Life is terminal. So enjoy and live your life, exploring your present situation at whatever stage. When we become elders, will others stop to aid us and steady our next steps? Time waits for no one; then again, waiting is all time does.

Why are we so obsessed with time as a society on Earth? Everything involves time. We set standards by time and have Standard Time and Daylight Savings Time. We gauge success and failure by time. There appears to be no escaping time anywhere on Earth, not in these so-called modern times.

"Oh my, but you were deep in thought, Just Kenja."

Pati'na, in her usual free-spirited perspective.

"You certainly weren't aware when I called you a second or the third time."

"Ya, sorry, I was just thinking, musing more than thinking."

"Anyway, Pati'na, what's up?"

"Come on, Just Kenja, let's go and explore today before it becomes tonight."

"Can you please call me only Kenja!"

"How many names do you have, Only Kenja?"

I was becoming more annoyed as I tried to clarify my intent when suddenly, the light went on.

Pati'na burst into teasing laughter while coyly dancing, saying she had been kidding with me all along since we first met.

"Okay, whatever Kenja you are today, let's go."

"Wait, shouldn't we eat something for breakfast first, Pati'na?"

"Are you hungry, Kenja?"

"No, I'm not hungry, but isn't it normal to start the day being nourished?"

"If you aren't hungry, you are fully nourished, Kenja."

I couldn't dispute her reasoning, considering that she now called me Kenja, which seemed more than enough of an accomplishment for this early in the day.

"We'll tell my parents that we plan to visit the Echoless Cave this morning, and I'll ask them for protection for today's adventure."

"Is this 'echoless' cave far from here, Pati'na?"

Pati'na started running ahead before she turned to say, "I can only know that when we get there."

From out of a stable, she appeared with her horse, a horse with no legs.

"Pati'na, your horse has no legs."

"I can see that, Kenja. It is my horse, after all, right."

"But how is it going to walk?"

"It'll walk like a horse with no legs, is how it will walk and always has walked."

"It's not like it is unique or anything, is it?"

"Here, can you help me strap on these water pouches?"

"Why the water pouches, Pati'na?"

"We'll need them to bring the dry-water back home to Ecaps."

I'm sure I must have looked bewildered, but 'dry-water' never really registered with me as I was still lost in thought, still working on being with a horse with no legs.

Seriously, how did I miss that? It's not as if the subject of 'dry-water' is part of an everyday conversation. Maybe it was my concern about all the missteps I took at the offset of my journeying yesterday. Still, it was evident that my focus remained elsewhere, not yet directed to the present moment. Focus, Kenja, focus.

I was taking in everything surrounding me while heading out on a trail and walking alongside a horse with no legs. This trail was similar to the one that led us to Ecaps yesterday, disregarding the horse with no legs, but how do you overlook walking with a horse with no legs?

The moisture coating the vegetation seemed different as we continued toward the cave. I couldn't place the reason I sensed this, but there was something different that I was missing.

Pati'na led the way to her favorite stream and then to Daydream Waterfalls, where she learned to cascade over the falls as a precaution when she was younger and safely endured the falls' menacing height.

We stopped as she showed me the villagers' watering system at Tangled Garden, which supplied continuous fresh produce for Ecaps and the surrounding communities. She mentioned we would stop on the way back to Ecaps to gather what her parents needed.

The more we traveled, the more I was mesmerized by Pati'na's youthful exuberance and naivety about any danger that might exist here. Yet I, too, felt no animosity lurking, none.

"We're nearing the cave entrance, Kenja."

"Watch your step, and there could be some Slugmucks about."

"A what? What's a Slugmuck?"

"It's sticky and mauve colored, and it might look like a flower, but one with no stem, just free-floating."

"They are not harmful, but touching them will lead you to believe things when they are not."

"Like hallucinating."

"If my description matches your hallucination, then yes."

I think and laugh to myself, *Right, how will I know? I'm walking with you, and a horse with no legs will retrieve some dry-water!*

"Here, take this and wash your hands. It will cleanse you."

"This looks like only water to me, no soap or sanitizer, Pati'na."

"It is water."

"But it doesn't feel wet."

"That's why we are here, Kenja, to collect more dry-water."

Well, it's becoming easy to appreciate that this morning will continue to become more intriguing by the minute. There is more happening here in these past few minutes than there would be in the final minutes of a tied hockey game in the playoffs.

"Did you say something, Kenja?"

# Deep Inside the Echoless Cave

"Are we nearly there? How much further, Pati'na?"

"It depends on where we are, Kenja."

Remembering how Pati'na teased me when I first arrived on Modeerf, when I asked, "Where are we?" And she teasingly replied, "We're here, you silly, Kenja." This time, it was my turn to do the teasing.

"We're here, you silly Pati'na."

Pati'na laughingly responded;

"Well, there seems to be nothing wrong with your memory, Kenja."

As we walked deeper into the landscape, the serenity continually impressed me. In Modeerf, there exists a consciousness that provides an inner sense of absolute safety. Even so, I felt that I had overlooked something obvious, but couldn't put my finger on it. Then, no pun intended, suddenly, the light went on.

There were no shadows, no shadows of any kind, and I had not seen a shadow anywhere since my arrival yesterday. At least, I think it was yesterday when I arrived because I hadn't seen a sunset last evening or a sunrise this morning. The peacefulness here was beyond enlightening and uniquely distinct from the tranquility I had experienced on my previous journeys or on Earth.

"Pati'na, Everything that I've seen so far, at least, would indicate that there may never be a need for medicines or medical miracles on Modeerf."

"You're reading way too much into your early observations, Kenja. This single-day experience of yours never tells the complete story. Give yourself more time and exposure for a more realistic, accountable life here on Modeerf."

Pati'na is starting to remind me more and more about one of my Grandmother, Dawnlilly's philosophies of never judging a book by its cover.

"Although, you did make me a little curious, Pati'na when you told me about learning how to escape danger by cascading down those threatening waterfalls. Yet you also indicated no impending dangers are common here."

"So, I'm a little confused. Which is it? Why would you need to escape something that isn't supposed to exist?"

"Here it is, Kenja, the entrance to the cave."

*This suddenness assured me that my answers would have to wait. By all indications, we have reached our intended destination.*

As I looked around, I saw only a pool of water, nothing remotely extraordinary. I quickly discovered it to be like good old, everyday normal water. What a neat way to disguise the entrance to the Echoless Cave containing the dry-water! I'm willing to bet this method of camouflage impresses my grandfather. Does he miss me yet?

"Quick, Kenja, follow me. Take my hand, and we'll jump before we're noticed."

"Who would notice us, and what about your horse?"

Mounting the horse with no legs, we jumped into the pool of water. Looking at everything happening now, I must have undoubtedly and unknowingly brushed up against one of those damn Slugmucks.

My instinct has always been to close my eyes when jumping into water. But this time, I begged my eyes to stay open, as I didn't want to miss a second of the experience this cave entranceway offered. I wasn't disappointed.

The pulsating energies of rapidly repeating lightning streaks and the sound of a roaring freight train thrust us forward with the force of a nuclear eruption, echoing violently for the duration of this transformation. I thought this was wild until I sensed this sharp, stabbing pain in my chest again, as I had earlier: It was becoming a concern.

In a short time, we resurfaced inside the Echoless Cave. I was disoriented, but once the depressurization from such an overwhelming eruption in my eardrums had diminished, with the return of my hearing, I listened. Still, there was only an acute and eerie dead silence.

Then, slowly emerging, it was there again—that enchanting, spellbinding, seductive music—the music that had caused me to ignore the increasing beat of the drumming, the drumming that announced the need to return from my journey. I totally and knowingly disregarded it, which was my third mistake in not abiding by the accepted practice of when to return from a journey.

This experience was certifiably mad. The cave was a monstrous, gigantic underground chambered area with many connecting caverns and a complex network of off-chutes extending from the main chamber. Countering the enormity of these stalactites were massive stalagmites resembling isotopes, teeming with energy. Could this energy be the creator of the spellbinding, enchanting music I first heard when entering Modeerf?

Is this why there is no sunrise or sunset, no extreme heat created by this massive build-up of energy? The ability of 'time' to be as long or as short as the thoughts in a moment. Could this synthetic form of light and heat be superior to our sun on Earth? Am I witnessing perpetual energy? So many questions.

My mind was reeling, and I was captivated, so what confused me? With these mind-boggling possibilities on full display, I contemplated the enormous potential in this 'powerhouse' of a cave. I began envisioning some staggering opportunities if this power source ever became available back on Earth.

Excitedly, I called out to Pati'na.

"Pati'na, do you realize what you have here on Modeerf? If I were to take this unbelievable power source back to earth."

Pati'na abruptly stopped me from finishing my thought and rather more than harshly replied.

"Attempting to do so would ensure your eternal stay here on Modeerf, Kenja, vaporizing any chance of you ever returning to your Earth."

Once again, in my life, where I think I am doing a good thing, well for others, I mess up, causing animosity and unwanted friction. Why can't I ever learn? Back home, my grandfather must be shaking his poor head in disbelief and wonderment.

One more self-inflicted wound registered. I tried to soothe the situation by discreetly changing the subject as we sat and rested the horse with no legs for a while before getting back to the task of retrieving a fresh supply of dry-water and delivering it to Ecaps.

"Pati'na, regarding your need to acquire a means of escaping an impending danger."

Oh, oh, once more, I triggered an unintended response.

"Why are you constantly questioning what you are experiencing here while journeying on Modeerf, Kenja? How can you possibly enjoy your journey? Insights are to be exposed, not opened for cross-examination."

"Pati'na, listen to my side. My journey ended when I ignored the drumming, signaling my return. I screwed up, triggering my torment and fear about the probability of ever returning home."

"No offense, but my quest is a quick one-man exodus from here back to Earth."

My lack of understanding of women didn't inhibit me from noticing an expression of doubt or regret on Pati'na's face.

While contemplating my communication shortcomings, I remember my grandfather's adage, "Try more often to look at the issue through the eyes of the examiner than just your own."

Ignoring things from Pati'na's perspective was a significant oversight on my part. The need for an apology was striking.

A solemn, sobering coolness now accompanied me as even the horse with no legs ignored my existence as we headed deeper into the Echoless Cave in pursuit of dry-water.

Once more, in an attempt to break this unintended iciness with Pati'na, I subtly asked.

"Pati'na, what is the significance of 'dry-water' here on Modeerf?"

I waited to see her reaction.

"I'm sorry, Kenja. What did you say?"

"I said that I think you are beautiful."

Shit, where the hell did that come from, you idiot! This is the last time I'm bringing my mouth along on a journey!

She turned slightly as if to respond and then seemed to think better of it. However, she exposed her face enough for me to see a curious glint in her eye and a partial smile. She neither acknowledged nor rejected what I had said.

I desperately tried to coyly engage in a new subject, stammering, and stuttering, attempting to recompose myself.

"Once we retrieve the dry-water, Pati'na, will we return to Ecaps tonight or wait until tomorrow morning?"

"We don't have a tomorrow on Modeerf, Kenja. We only have today, always today, in the now. We have yesterdays but no tomorrows."

Okay, this is better. Please take a deep breath and try to at least think before moving your lips, but Pati'na is seemingly engaging with me again. I cautiously continue, hoping I remain standing on a little firmer ground and off that quagmire I've created.

"Okay, I can appreciate that, Pati'na, but what about the dry-water? What is its importance, and why does it appear critically vital to your people?"

"Short answer, Kenja, we need the dry-water to survive and prevent disease. Another significant property of dry-water is its ability to decelerate the aging process substantially."

"Pati'na, where I come from, you have just described the 'Utopia of all Elixir'. This would be the best thing since sliced bread."

"Sliced bread. I'm sorry, Kenja, I don't understand what you are trying to tell me."

"No, no, I am sorry, Pati'na. Please continue."

I can envision my grandfather telling my Grandmother Dawnlilly that he's seen enough and is going fishing.

Pati'na looked scornfully at me and looked me squarely in the eyes.

"Now listen to me, Kenja, I'm going to spell this out to you line by line. Are you listening? The dry-water exists solely here, Kenja, in this Echoless Cave. It catalyzes the energy-icicles to keep functioning, producing infinite energy. This formula continues to be the most sought-after throughout this universe."

"Kenja, look at me and listen."

"Kenja, are you listening?"

"You will never return to your Earth if you should ever obtain this knowledge or even if the Unknowns might suspect that you possess the ability to locate this cave."

"You will be pursued relentlessly till your death."

"Do you understand?"

"Tell me you understand."

"Yes, I get it, Pati'na. I am fully aware of what you are telling me."

Damn, how do I walk into these situations repeatedly, even when I know what will happen, even visualizing the outcomes beforehand? I do it anyway. My grandfather will surely be, once again, shaking his head if he hasn't already left to go fishing.

"Can you tell me one more thing, Pati'na? How do you know where the dry-water will be found in such a massive complex?"

"I don't know how to find the dry-water, Kenja."

"You're kidding, right?"

"Then why did we come here if you can't find this dry-water?"

"I can't find it, but my horse with no legs can."

"You look serious."

"Are you serious? You look serious."

"I'm much more than serious, Kenja."

"This method has been our way of concealing the identity of who possesses the means to the dry-water's location since the beginning of our civilization."

"Seriously, Pati'na, it's been a horse with no legs all this time."

"Now that's mad."

"Seriously mad."

"I'm sorry, Kenja. What are you saying?"

"Again, I don't understand what you are trying to tell me."

"No, this is good, Pati'na. Although it is seriously mad, a good, insane mad."

"And by all accounts, without a doubt, the 'Mother-Load' of being mad."

Pati'na looked bewilderingly at Kenja before opting to continue.

"This has been our way of identifying dry-water, faithfully passed down from generation to generation."

"Today, this responsibility belongs to my beloved horse, Eaus'eche."

"Kenja, the 'Unknowns 'have always mocked my horse Eaus'eche, even doubting my love and care for her, sometimes questioning her usefulness, unaware that she held the key to identifying dry-water."

Although we had managed to progress deep into the farthest extremities of this Echoless Cave, finding any dry-water had eluded Eaus'eche to this point. I was beginning to suspect this dry-water was elusive, even in Modeerf searching with a horse with no legs.

"Kenja, you must be projecting positive intentions inside this cave, and Kenja, my senses indicate otherwise."

What is it with these female senses and intuitions?

"This negative doubting you are continually expressing will interfere with her capability to locate the only source of dry-water."

"Just be positive for once."

If I ever go back home, I must examine my deep cynicism. Compared to what I witness here, where there is a display of trust, an unsuspicious, almost childlike existence.

The cave remained reasonably well-lit as we continued carefully traveling further in our search, with no evidence of artificial lighting. Oddly, this lighting cast no shadows. Even the horse with no legs was shadow-free. Come to think of it, I haven't seen a watch, a clock, or any other means of telling time anywhere.

Eaus'eche's sudden whining while excitingly tossing her head about brought me back to the present moment and the reality of this search for the dry-water. What I once thought was a sorry exercise in futility while searching for this elusive dry-water now appeared to become a reality.

Any doubts I might have harbored were quickly dispelled as I bent to touch what was indeed dry-water. Elation quickly filled the many chambers of this Echoless Cave with booming jubilation as Pati'na, and I prepared to replenish the two dry-water pouches straddling Eaus'eche's back.

"Kenja, this is important. You must understand the process."

"Kenja, please stop nodding and please just listen."

"You must handle these water pouches with great care."

"Kenja, stop looking around and listen to me. Just try to focus, okay."

That was easy for her to say, but this place was utterly unbelievable.

"These next steps are vital for the safety and storage of transporting dry-water from here to the Storage Facility in Ecaps."

I looked directly at Pati'na, trying my best to pay attention, but considering and contending with all of the existing distractions, concentration was, at best, limited.

"Good, Kenja, that's good, keep that focus."

"This product is quite stable while remaining in this Echoless Cave's environment. The same conditions exist inside the water pouches used during its transportation, as does the Storage Facility in Ecaps."

She gave me that look only a woman has, which means, 'I know that you're not listening'.

"Transporting dry-water via any other means outside of this Echoless Cave before it has been processed at the facility, in any other type of vessel, would lead to a catastrophic disaster, resulting in an explosion that would challenge the original big bang, altering the dynamics of the universe itself.”

The seriousness of Pati'na's words was not lost on me, as back home on Earth, this possibility of a nuclear disaster often seemed possible, an accident in the making. Usually, it is no longer considered an 'If 'in some facilities, but only a 'When'.

Acknowledging the seriousness of the moment but also being curious about this relatively small amount of water to sustain Ecaps, even with it being a special kind of dry-water, I asked Pati'na, “Will these two water pouches supply your village's needs, including the remaining communities on Modeerf, for very long? It doesn't seem nearly adequate, not really, not from my perspective.”

“Kenja, understandably, you are comparing it with ordinary water. Once processed at the facility, the unique properties of dry-water are that a few drops are equivalent to an enormous reservoir. It is that potent and even more remarkable in its numerous usages.”

With Pati'na and the horse with no legs now leading the way, we started meandering among the numerous options leading toward the Echoless Cave's exit;

I imagined being a gallant Roman legionnaire, a glorified centurion returning from a crusade and marching home to Ecaps after a victorious expedition with the Emperor's Quest in hand.

Then I thought, *Give it a rest, Kenja; this 'gallant' fantasy is nothing compared to what you're experiencing now with Pati'na on Modeerf.*

I could sense my grandfather finally smiling while baiting his hook back home in Witchenbrook.

# The Unknowns

As soon as we left the cave, it dawned on me that I had no recollection of how we managed to find our way out. It was reminiscent of those times back on Earth when I would drive along a familiar road, and the right side of my brain would get the left side to keep us safe and continue operating. At the same time, the right side of my brain would drift off into a realm of daydreams.

Then something would snap me back to the present moment, and if asked, I couldn't tell you anything I might have recently passed or even seen, as Pati'na's voice had done just now.

"Look, Kenja. These are some signs of the Unknowns, so they've been here recently. These signs are never good at any time, but right now, I can't warn my family and the others."

"Can't you use that beacon you mentioned, Pati'na?"

"No, once the Unknowns have entered an area, they have a device, some negative energy field, preventing the transfer of our beacon. Unfortunately, one we've never been able to counteract fully, at least not yet."

We continued the journey back to Ecaps with a little more caution and awareness of our surroundings, becoming more alert to any abnormalities along the way.

"Pati'na, how did these Unknowns ever end up the way they are today?"

"Our elders teach that they have been a part of Modeerf since its creation. Like all other communities, the original Unknowns reflected and mirrored their passive cooperative nature, contributing to the betterment of all on Modeerf. From ancient times, Kenja, Modeerf has been a peaceful place where all living things coexist and share the benefits of equal potential opportunities.”

As we neared a windfall, Pati’na hitched Eaus’eche to a broken branch and motioned to sit on the nearby fallen tree; once we were seated, she continued.

“In hard times, strange and disturbing activities began when things were out of balance. One of these involved my cousin, Vexiana, who had grown to distrust her Fate-Keepers so much that she began questioning their wisdom and motives even more alarmingly. She revolted, siding with some of the more radical and distrusting of the Unknowns.”

Pati’na slowly shakes her head, mimicking disbelief.

“Vexiana ignored the obvious to indulge herself, joining the Unknowns, at this time led by a group of vengeful Males leading the Unknowns. Vexiana’s dream was becoming a vengeful force among them. These events deeply hurt me, Kenja.”

Pati’na’s expression of sadness at being broken-hearted was evident.

“With our mothers being sisters, Vexiana was not only my cousin and best friend, but our resemblance to each other was quite uncanny. Others would have easily assumed we were twin sisters, possibly identical twins. We were inseparable when we were young, often pretending to be each other, having fun tricking people.”

Pausing momentarily, with a tear running down her cheek, quietly sniffling, Pati’na continued relating past events.

“So to watch how Vexiana’s conversion to this maligned vision of the Unknowns was horrible for me to accept, Kenja.”

“It does sound dreadful, Pati’na. I can feel your pain as you speak.”

“This marginal group severed ties, breaking away into a sect, Kenja.”

Her body language mockingly suggested that it was no big deal when it first happened.

"At first, most citizens of Unknowns largely ignored the vengeful group. This allowed them to gain power, dominate, and carry out their disturbing intentions without opposition. This left little option for the remaining members of Unknowns to join us in Ecaps. Unfortunately, this breakaway sect was left to its own devices, resulting in a regrettable outcome."

Pati'na stood to find a more comfortable spot to sit on the old fallen tree and then continued.

"Some of my other friends were sadly converted as well, but none so hurtful as Vexiana's. My father, Sawenco, and a few other elders became concerned about where all this was heading as the Unknowns' lies became more and more unbelievable; as their lies became more blatant, the number of people following their lead increased proportionally."

"Then Ecaps Chief of Council held a series of information Town Hall meetings attempting to bring awareness and discredit these Unknowns, to no avail. There seemed to be no bottom to their repulsive behavior, and nothing seemed to ever be below them."

As I watched Pati'na speak, I could see how much the situation weighed on her. She kept wringing her hands and making nervous gestures as she talked, showing how burdened she felt.

"The more profound their untruths, the more their numbers increased, Kenja. You see, these untruths, in their eyes, weren't untruths at all, so in their mind, they didn't lie because, oddly enough, somehow their untruths had become their reality. Perhaps only in their minds, but these untruths spread faster and deeper than gossip in Modeerf."

"But Pati'na, surely these people could see how they were being manipulated to appease someone's deranged, damaging beliefs, never mind these seemingly sick philosophies with these out-and-out lies?"

"Kenja, even by dispelling the public untruths and theories of the rebellious Unknowns, with the erosion of the serenity broken, and the trust that had existed for eons on Modeerf vaporizing, now placing this trust in the vault of yesterday."

"This episode was originally a minor occurrence, but a simple misunderstanding left free to fester eventually challenged the existence of Modeerf constantly. A price we continue to pay to this day, Kenja."

"What about these signs you mentioned, these signs of the Unknowns, showing they were here recently?"

"How do you see these signs anyway, Pati'na? I didn't see anything obvious. Why can't I see these signs, too?"

"I think it would be best to sit again and talk, Kenja."

"It may take me a while to explain this to you, and hopefully, I don't complicate it any more than it already is."

We found a decent place to take a break, and this time, we gave the horse with no legs and ourselves a chance to rest more comfortably. Then, Pati'na continued.

"After this sect of Unknowns broke away, and with them now proclaiming to represent all of the Unknowns, these events eventually established a crack in the fragility of Modeerf itself. This sect separated, having lost access to dry-water necessary for survival. They needed to find a substitute for this essential element in their diet to maintain good health in their now isolated existence."

"This couldn't have been an easy thing to do, Pati'na."

"No, it wasn't, Kenja, not at all. After extensive research into substituting the essential dry-water properties, they discovered the only available food source to fill the void: the mintberry. But it wasn't quite as simple as consuming some of these Mintberries or drinking mintberry juice; this action alone would never sustain good health for most people's well-being."

"But, Pati'na, how could they be sure that this slim, at best, possibility even had a chance?"

"That's a good question, Kenja, because they didn't know. The Council of the Unknowns mandated, without exception, that everyone consume the berries, leaves, and roots of the mintberry tree as part of their diet. Their research confirmed that its properties, although seemingly completely tasteless, appeared to be sufficient in establishing the necessary nutritional balance. One of our elders, Paneta, our Medicinal Maker, made it her mission, her lifelong ambition, to create a means of detecting their presence and warning of their impending threat or danger.”

“So, Pati’na, this fact of how essential the mintberry was became the catalyst in Paneta’s research?”

“Exactly, Paneta recognized the mintberry’s importance to the Unknowns’ well-being. To develop a trigger for detecting their presence and whereabouts, she used the properties of the mintberry as a catalyst and building block.”

Pati’na paused momentarily as Eaus’eche seemed agitated by something, being only flying insects, nothing threatening.

“Paneta’s hybrid research established a means of detecting the Unknowns ’presence every time they exhaled by using a type of fern, the Maidenhair fern, growing extensively around Ecaps and throughout most territories on Modeerf.”

“Wow, this sounds fascinating, like an old movie plot but a complicated one, at least to me; it sounds complicated, Pati’na.”

“To me too, Kenja, but Paneta’s brilliance allowed her research to eventually reveal how the exposed Maidenhair fern would react to the slightest presence of the Mintberries properties.”

“So if I understand, Pati’na, whenever Unknowns exhaled nearby a Maidenhair fern, it would become stimulated on its underside?”

“Exactly, taking on a grayish glow that became visible only to those vaccinated with Paneta’s detection and identification serum, to which the Unknowns were unaware, let alone ever having access.”

“Can I be vaccinated with Paneta’s serum, Pati’na?”

“Unfortunately, Kenja, it is only beneficial to the people created on this land of Modeerf.”

There it was again, ‘created’, not born? My Grandfather WiKenja taught me not to interrupt when someone is speaking, so I’ll wait for the right moment to ask more about it.

"I'm sorry to hear this, Pati'na, but are the signs of their presence an immediate threat right now?"

"Not immediate, Kenja, but it is still very concerning that they managed to get this close to discovering the existence of the Echoless Cave, never mind the treasure it holds."

We had only traveled a short distance from the Echoless Cave when it became apparent that the Unknowns were in the area more by chance than by any conceived plan, as indicated by the openness of where they had stopped to rest, drink, and water their animals.

During our walk back home to Ecaps, I felt a sense of inner peace, knowing we had accomplished the primary objective. Even so, I concluded that as much as Modeerf was grounded in this coveted air of stability and contentment, it was as fragile as any other egg incubating into something more significant.

Having traveled what I perceived as halfway back to Ecaps, I suggested that we sit and rest briefly once more, as again, I was tiring so easily and much more quickly than I should have been. Pati'na watered the horse with no legs again and then joined me, resting on an old stump.

"Kenja, can you tell me a few things about your Earth while we sit here?"

"Well, what sort of things, Pati'na?"

"Little odd things found on your Earth."

"First, it's not my Earth. Besides, just hearing you say that alone seems odd."

Turning around, I'm looking at a horse with no legs, one who controls the secret to this planet's future existence, and you want to know some oddities on Earth.

"Well, Pati'na, one always stuck out to me: how we put a misplaced value on some things on Earth. Individuals sometimes receive no monetary reward for their beneficial contributions to humanity during their lifetime. Then a movie company will pay an actor millions of dollars to perform and act portraying the life of this very person, who often, in real life, lived their entire life in obscurity, often in poverty."

"That does seem odd, Kenja."

"Can you tell me a few more before we head home?"

"We could live here for all of eternity, Pati'na, and there wouldn't be enough time to come to the bottom of this infinite list of Earth's oddities. But, another would be how we can accept some things we can't see but acknowledge them as existing, things like the wind, love, hope, trust, faith, and air among many, and then can look at something so evident as being the truth and yet deny it, things like that. Much like your discussion about the Unknowns."

"Oh, and sometimes one word can be interpreted differently, often dividing people. One clear example I can think of is the word 'smudge' Pati'na."

Typically, 'smudge' carries a negative undertone such as impurity, contamination, or dirtiness, often suggesting that something of value has been tarnished. However, to those with a Native Aboriginal background, 'smudge' or 'smudging' refers to a method of purification or cleansing using sage and sweetgrass smoke.

"I would like to learn more about your Earth, Kenja, but we should start heading back now with the dry-water before our absence causes concern."

We began our journey back to Ecaps, giving me more time to appreciate what this fantastic land of Modeerf has already revealed, lessons learned, and philosophies exposed. Its much-untold paranormal intellect is yet to be explored and benefited from.

After settling back into my cocoon-shaped hammock in Ecaps, I reflected on everything this day had revealed. I considered the lessons I had learned, the truths about my behavior that this day had unmasked, and what, if anything, was most important to share with my grandfather.

As I meditated, clearing my mind, the answer became clear about what held the most significance. I recognized Pati'na's horse, the one with no legs, and her role as the guardian of Ecaps.

Grandfather, today's lesson, as exposed by Eaus'eche, is that *first impressions are not always the best impressions.*

# Hannah Takes Control

Slowly opening my eyes, I see that nothing much has changed since I fell asleep last night, again, if there is a night. Listening brought awareness, one more oddity: no songbirds were filling the morning air; not only that, I had yet to see an insect.

Walking slowly and quietly, noting what was around me and, more so, what was not, I noticed Pati'na heading my way.

"Hi, Kenja. What would you like to do today?"

"I'm not really clear on the Unknowns, and knowing the situation between you and your cousin Vexiana, I don't want to provoke any negative issues for you, Pati'na, but there seems more to this story."

"There is more to tell. Do you have any thoughts as to where you would like me to start? Kenja?"

"You mentioned that your cousin joined the breakaway sect of the Unknowns because of her distrust of her Fate-Keepers, and she reached out to radical members of the Unknowns. Who were these people?"

"During that period, the Unknowns were mainly governed by a trio of men and a council comprising five male members. However, it may be overstating things to say they were truly leading; floundering and faulting would be more accurate terms. The Klongs' continuous attack resulted in the deaths of many people and left others greatly unsettled, resulting in these Unknown leaders relocating their people to their newly fortified community. Unfortunately, things only worsened as a lack of faith in their leadership and the ongoing lack of access to dry-water began to take its toll."

"But, they had the mintberry to fall back on, right?"

"It wasn't nearly enough to replace nor sustain dry-water properties over the long run, Kenja."

"Two things happened almost at the same time. Upon her arrival at the Unknowns village, Vexiana was befriended by a woman named Hannah, her husband Erlude, and their two young children, along with the continuing unrest between the people of Unknowns and their lack of confidence for their very survival with the current leadership."

"Vexiana often looked after these two children while Erlude and Hannah gathered Mintberries and helped process the mintberry properties. The availability of these berries continued to diminish as the need for additional nutrition increased"

"It sounds like it was quite the struggle simply staying alive, Pati'na."

"That's exactly what happened, Kenja. Over time, so many of the Unknowns became malnourished and died from their situation. Sadly, Vexiana had to witness Vexiana's husband, Erlude, and both of Hannah's two young children agonizingly die of malnutrition. Many other families also endured the tragic loss of children, with many of the elderly wretchedly succumbing."

"This situation got to the boiling point when people started secretly meeting, knowing that without advocating on their own behalf, there would inevitably be more people perishing and civil unrest assured to follow. The moment that changed the leadership and direction of the Unknowns occurred when Hannah and other women who had lost family members to the misguided decisions of their leaders revolted. They overthrew the established leaders and gained a substantial following, soon becoming the governing body for the Council of the Unknowns."

"During this uprising, it became evident that Hannah was the go-to person for the other women. Hannah didn't openly embrace this; there were few other options. Even though Hannah and her fellow council members improved living conditions for the Unknowns, particularly for the women and children, creating an evenly balanced distribution of all available commodities. Hannah knew that without access to dry-water, the existing nutritional values were insufficient for a prolonged existence."

"To say that Hannah was Vexiana's hero would only be touching the surface. Hannah helped provide Vexiana with her living quarters and encouraged her in all her undertakings. Hannah's decision to have Vexiana remain at arm's length from all the political committees allowed her to speak openly with Vexiana about any concerns or issues free of conflict of interest."

"Wow, that's quite a transition, Pati'na. And wise of Hannah to have the foresight to keep her friendship with Vexiana separate from politics."

"It was, Kenja. But one that unfortunately is probably destined to cause more chaos unless these Unknowns can return to their former ways and rejoin Ecaps and the other communities living in harmony, as we share access to the dry-water."

"And you don't think this will ever happen, Pati'na?"

"Once you drop crystal, the wholeness is shattered for all eternity, Kenja."

"On a brighter note, Kenja. Would you like to come along with me and Eaus'eche as we are heading out this morning to replenish our dry-water supply?"

"Let me pack up a few things, and I'll meet you at the stables, Pati'na."

# Achieving Success

There was that glint again in Pati'na's eyes, the twinkle that had been absent since our morning outing when replenishing the dry-water supply. With the task now completed and the dry-water safely stored, Ecaps had a festive atmosphere.

I was looking forward to having a laid-back afternoon, just relaxing, as I felt uncomfortably tired again.

"Come on, Kenja. If you're up to it, let's seize the remainder of the day and explore the boundaries of Puzzle Lake and the lookout up on Dispute Ridge."

*It was nice to see Pati'na display her spontaneous laughter again. But why would she mention my energy level unless it has become more apparent?*

But, there was that enticing glint, easily overriding my speculation. I watched Pati'na amusingly dance toward the stables, picking up Eaus'eche's favorite horse blanket, draping this cooler across her back, and slowly walking back toward the stables. After being hosed down and groomed, Eaus'eche was given water, oats, and fresh hay and returned to her stall.

Pati'na turned toward me while laughing and smiling, saying enthusiastically.

"Now, my friend, 'whatever-your-name-is-today'."

"We're free to roam, explore and enjoy."

"Let's go, Kenja."

Pati'na suggested we visit the lookout up on Dispute Ridge first, where we could look down over the majestic beauty of the lake from above, taking in all it offered.

The ridge was utterly remarkable, with an incredible view of Puzzle Lake. Soon, I was using my favorite expression when something overwhelmed me.

"This is mad, Pati'na. This is absolutely mad. I hope you're seeing what I'm seeing."

Once more, Pati'na displayed delight, laughingly saying, "I don't know, Kenja, is what you're seeing, mad."

Witnessing her frolicking nature on full display again was a welcoming sight. The only thing more beautiful in my line of vision from all on display around me was Pati'na herself. And even though the beauty around me was remarkable, it paled in comparison.

"Let's go to the lake now, Kenja."

"We'll fly down."

*Whoa, fly down? Hold up a minute; she did say fly down. I haven't seen a plane or, for that matter, an airport since arriving here in Modeerf, so this suggestion takes me back slightly.*

"And how do you propose we do that, my young Miss Pati'na?"

"What do you mean, how, my brave knight?"

"Like I said, how?"

"We jump off the ridge and fly. How difficult can that be for you, Sir Knight?"

"I think you better go back to calling me Just Kenja because I have no idea what you are talking about. Jump off and fly. Do you think so? More like jump off and 'splat' you die to me."

I watched in disbelief, and to my horror, Pati'na leaped from the cliff only to soon begin soaring as free as a bird. I looked around to see if any nasty little Slugmucks might lurk about, altering my perception of what I witnessed.

No, this was happening as Pati'na came swooping overhead with the glee of an infant taking its first step in life. Her exuberance showered me with awe and disbelief.

"Come on, Kenja, learn to fly; believe in yourself. Open your door to the wonders we all unknowingly possess. Take that literal leap of faith. Come and fly with me into these shared realms of possibilities."

"Oh, and Kenja, this is 'Mad, Holy Shit Mad'!"

Without one iota of doubt and with eyes wide open, I next felt the thrill of being accompanied only by the wind. Ascending skyward, the unimaginable became as natural as breathing.

Watching Pati'na hovering beside me, laughingly;

"Well, my brave Sir Knight, welcome to the Land of Imagination, where anything becomes everything, where dreams become realities."

It felt like we had soared above any existing reality and beyond the clouded horizon into infinity.

"This is madness, Pati'na, crazy fantastic madness."

"And, yes, this is Holy shit madness!"

I quickly went from being a fledgling to becoming a curious, confident bird of prey. If only my grandfather could see me now, flying as majestic as a Hawk.

We were like two little kids having a pillow fight, the way we chased and pranked each other. We were filled with laughter and bewilderment, sharing wonderment and awe. It was one of those moments that would end too soon, even if it lasted forever.

We circled around Puzzle Lake before landing on the beautiful white sand beach. Pati'na seemed to be completely absorbed in the experience and looked like she belonged there.

"Kenja, I think we'll find more madness in the waters of Puzzle Lake," as she stripped naked and dove into the crystal-clear waters.

# Meeting the Gatekeeper

Most days in Modeerf's mid-summer didn't vary much, differing from tepid to perhaps subtropical climate in Ecaps and the mainland. In the distance, I could see the inspiring white caps of the neighboring mountains, which, if given a chance, I would so much like to visit.

There was a buzz around the village this morning with the garden vegetables being ready for harvesting, and plans were devised for who would do what, where, and when. Kenja watched Pati'na, her mother, Yada, many other women, and some of the older girls from the village heading out to Tangled Garden for the harvest.

It was another typical morning in Ecaps. Young children attended the local schools, and many proprietors opened their places of business and workplaces for another day. This slow, quiet pace is reminiscent of the one I fondly remembered while living with my grandparents in Witchenbrook.

Noticing Jonfrei, the Pathfinder, heading toward a trail largely unused by the vegetation discouraging its access. I called out, "Can I join you, Jonfrei?"

While hoping for a positive response, adding,

"I have nothing to do here today, and I might assist you."

I did not have a clue as to how I might assist Jonfrei.

"I don't think that would be advisable, Kenja," Jonfrei replied.

"This particular trail leads to the main route maintained by the Unknowns, constantly patrolled and strictly enforced."

"The penalty is the same whether for intentional or accidental trespassing."

"I do appreciate that, Jonfrei, but even so, I have been hoping to speak with you for some time now about finding myself stranded here on Modeerf and if there might be a way for me to return to Earth."

Jonfrei was a skilled and capable person with a deep understanding of things that no one else seemed to know about. I really needed his knowledge if I ever wanted to leave the place called Modeerf.

"It will be a long walk to reach my destination, Kenja, where I have a personal concern while hoping to learn more of this mystic mountain's mysteries."

"You can accompany me until we reach that point where the terrain gets much more forbidding and challenging."

"If you agree to that, then come along and be quick of it."

I grabbed my walking staff, which Pati'na's father Sawenco had made for me. I am grateful for this opportunity to share time alone with Jonfrei and quickly catch up with him.

As I attempted to keep up with Jonfrei's quick pace and still trying to make conversation simultaneously, I realized my energy levels were, at a minimum, more than simply subpar.

"Have you always been a Pathfinder, Jonfrei?"

I watched his facial expression to see whether he might be open to engaging with me or more content to be lost in his thoughts.

"No, before this, I wasn't a Pathfinder, Kenja."

I received a response to a question that didn't answer what I sought. It reminded me of my brother's friend Larry, a lawyer who tends to give vague answers. It was frustrating that there was no small talk or lead-in to help me achieve what I sought.

"So, Jonfrei, was your father the Pathfinder before you?"

"My father was and still is our Gatekeeper here on Modeerf, Kenja. He has been our Gatekeeper even before my creation."

That was an intriguing fact I only recently had become aware of, being created, not born, on Modeerf. It was a fascination. I would like to explore this process further, but I must remain focused on my quest to find a means of departing here for home to Earth.

Unexpectedly, Jonfrei continued our conversation as we walked, "Kenja, today my father needs a Gatekeeper as his light dims. However, identifying Ecaps's future Gatekeeper hasn't happened."

I watched his eyes searching the horizon, carefully choosing his words.

"My father feels incapable of fulfilling his daily duties while his health fails. And now unassisted and alone, becoming uncharacteristically anxious about his death."

"So, is this why you seem to be callously venturing into the Unknowns territory and exploring this particular mountain?"

"What is the name of this mountain, Jonfrei?"

Sensing my question is easily dismissed, at present being of no concern.

The further we traveled, the more Jonfrei looked downcast and disheartened, resembling a man wholly depleted of any reason to go on. He was cloaked in this desperation surrounding him as we walked.

As our muted journey led us through this lush tropical rainforest, thick with moss and ferns, we continued putting one foot before the other. Watching his struggling movements, even this minor impediment appeared to be challenging.

Jonfrei broke the silence, "We have reached the limits of our journey together, Kenja, with it becoming much more precarious from this point forward, so I strongly suggest, no, I insist that you now return to Ecaps,"

I sensed that little voice inside me suggesting that continuing this journey together was in our best interests.

"Before we part, Jonfrei, could you tell me how you started your occupation as Pathfinder?"

As I take the initial step forward, I hope Jonfrei will do likewise.

"It's not an occupation, Kenja."

Jonfrei stood still, hesitating.

"I was chosen the Pathfinder, as my father, Roulen, was the Gatekeeper."

Perhaps unaware, Jonfrei began slowly walking.

"We are not immortal, but longevity in our positions has happened because of dry-water here and its particular properties."

As we spoke, I continued walking along the trail beside Jonfrei. I wasn't fooling him; he could have ended this walk at any point.

"So, Jonfrei, your intent is what?"

I was gesturing with my hands.

"To find your father assisting him in his hour of need?"

Jonfrei's expression indicated I was close to ending our conversation and potentially being dismissed. Momentarily, he continued.

"I received word that my father was seen in the lower quarter of the mountain. People who saw him recognized him as my father, and it made them sad to see him wandering around, chasing what seemed to be a ghost or an illusion. He appeared confused and lost in thought, searching for something he only believed existed."

As we hiked up the trail, the temperature began to drop. Leaving the warm, humid rainforest behind, I sensed a developing issue.

I asked Jonfrei. "About the temperature, Jonfrei, we don't seem to be dressed for the weather we'll encounter while ascending this mountainside, right?"

"Listen, don't you think we should make a plan or something?"

"Are you getting cold, Kenja?"

"Aren't you?"

"No."

This was another blunt and direct answer, with no hint of an offer to resolve my impending concern, which, up to this point, I had attempted to disguise as a request vainly.

"Well, I am getting quite concerned as surely the temperature will only fall further as we climb higher, Jonfrei."

"Tell your mind to ignore your senses of this problematic situation, Kenja."

Bloody hell, 'this problematic situation'. Death is much more than a problematic situation. Of course, I could always do as suggested, and then perhaps Jonfrei's father, Roulen, the Gatekeeper, will miraculously appear. I will undoubtedly require his services in my final hours.

"I knew having you come along was going to be a mistake, and it seems that you are going out of your way to prove it, Kenja."

"I don't have time for this, Kenja"

"You don't have time for this?"

"You don't have time for this, Jonfrei!"

"Agreed, now let's move on, Kenja."

"Nice winter parka, by the way, good choice."

I was warm, but I didn't dare look.

Jonfrei seemed to be struggling with more than just confusion, and I wondered if it was due to stress or exhaustion. Although I had seen similar symptoms at high elevations, we were not at that high an altitude. I gently placed my hand on his shoulder and suggested he take a break and rest briefly.

"Jonfrei, I understand that you are searching for your father and, unfortunately, have not had much success."

Kenja was now standing directly in front of Jonfrei.

"I suggest having faith in your soul and allowing it to reach out and communicate with your father's soul."

"The first flaw in your theory, Kenja, is that here on Modeerf, we don't have a soul."

Now, I was becoming more than a little irritated:

"Listen, Jonfrei, if I can walk with a horse with no legs, fly like a Hawk, walk on raging rapids, swim with the Cuffers while breathing underwater, talk to the Little People, and now, now I'm wearing the most comfortable parka I have ever worn. Don't you dare sit there and tell me you can't feel your soul?"

Kenja stood before him, scolding him as a parent might scold a stubborn child.

"Now feel your damn soul and tell it to find your father's."

Momentarily, out of sheer frustration, screaming, "Now!"

After taking a deep breath and considering Jonfrei's circumstances, I feared that, once again, I may have demanded too much from someone who has given it their all, as I have often done in my hockey coaching career.

"Stand up, Jonfrei, search the heavens, and follow your soul. It's possible that your father has finally discovered his soul, which he may have previously experienced but never acknowledged due to the people's beliefs on Modeerf. This newfound realization could be confusing him and your father's soul has been preparing him to die so he can be released to travel to the afterlife for eternity. This foreign experience greatly challenges him."

We continued cautiously scouring the mountain's steep sides, with their jagged overhanging bluffs and sharply carved ridges, while continuously inching our way higher toward the summit.

Our quest had made it very clear that we were searching for someone's life to help it receive death.

The trail disappeared, fading into the mountainside as we scaled steep ledges with uneven, treacherous footing, just waiting for its opportunity to strike out.

This adventure is more befitting a young, experienced mountaineer; not for me in my present state of becoming tired so quickly, and, it seemed, not for Jonfrei, whose legs now reminded me of a newborn calf standing for the first time, shaking and trembling as it tried to remain upright.

I, too, became more concerned with this repeating pang in my chest, not as sharp as before, yet still not feeling quite myself.

"Let's rest here for a moment, Jonfrei. You can share more about your father with me, and perhaps this will stimulate your soul with its need to connect with your intention of communicating with his soul."

I tried to distract Jonfrei from his current situation by talking about his father and what might have caused him to reach that point.

"Every time my father assisted someone walking their path to arrive at their gate, a little piece of himself would seem to die, too."

"Accumulating these losses over such a long period has significantly affected his well-being, Kenja."

Jonfrei slowly stood, becoming alert as his eyes scanned, searching.

"I can feel him, Kenja."

He seemed hopeful while being shrouded with a blanket of sadness.

"We are very near him."

Not wanting to interrupt Jonfrei's connection, I silently followed my desperate, exhausted friend as he became open to his new sense of having a soul.

We soon discovered Roulen further up the mountain, climbing to a significantly higher mountain segment than expected.

After huddling together in Roulen's shelter and checking on his condition, Jonfrei explained his intention to his father to return him to Ecaps, where assistance would be available.

"Come, father. Kenja and I will assist you down from this mountain to Ecaps."

"My dear son Jonfrei, I do not need to go down the mountain, as you have brought my Gatekeeper with you today."

"Listen to me, my son. I once overheard Kenja speak to Pati'na about his soul, and I came to this mountain in search of and found mine."

Now Roulen began shaking Kenja's hand, offering thanks.

"Not down the mountain, Jonfrei."

He began holding Jonfrei in the palm of his hands.

"This is my time to have scaled the mountain to my destiny."

Slowly nodding his head, Roulen concluded, "My life is now to become part of the infinity of endless eternity by releasing my soul, setting it free."

Then, with his final breath, "To my final journey on the face of my mountain, Gate-Keepers Mountain."

# The Spirit of the Wind

Roulen's breathing had become inconsistent and fainter than it had been early in the morning. His physical weakness indicated his death to be near at hand. I watched his face and eyes shut, yet he seemed to smile at something or someone only he could see.

He continuously took the edge of his blanket, curling it tightly into a wad and tugging it up to his face. His eyelids remained closed, yet I witnessed his shut, restless eyes, constantly looking about, steadily roaming, scanning, and observing what was apparently only visible to him.

My Grandmother Dawnlilly displayed these very similar actions the day she prepared to die. The understanding is that when we are nearing our death, our soul temporarily leaves our body to take flight and practice for its journey ahead.

As witnessed in the fall, when birds congregate, they take flight with their young, practicing for days, teaching them the patterns needed and how to manage the long-enduring distances ahead. Once the elders are confident that the young have become competent and familiar with their demands, they take flight to their destination.

I believed Roulen had been watching and smiling as his soul practiced for its pending journey, which appeared well-prepared for its departure.

Roulen's last breath was not a sad moment, dying in his son's arms high on Gate-Keepers Mountain.

Roulen was visibly far from the fear we first encountered when finding him. Roulen's current facile expression will stay with me forever. His skin tone became young again, seemingly free of wrinkles. His eyes and lips emitted a warm satisfaction.

My last words spoken to Roulen were, "May the Spirit of the Wind see you through the Fog."

How can this possibly be interpreted as a sad or solemn experience? It wasn't.

We temporarily buried Roulen, with both of us completely exhausted, unable to return his remains to the village of Ecaps. Carefully marking the site's location so the recovery party could locate his remains on Gate-Keepers Mountain, we started descending toward the rainforest's warmer temperate zone, now too consumed to appreciate the wonders Gate-Keepers Mountain offered.

Jonfrei likely reflected on the journeys he had previously shared with his father and how short they must seem today. While walking along this now perceived lifeless trail, we spoke only a few words, as talk was no longer necessary.

By late afternoon, we reached the warmer temperatures where the cocoa and nut trees grew. For the first time since Roulen passed away, I sensed the warmth of my surroundings. I refocused, becoming conscious of being in the present moment.

Jonfrei suggested we camp and rest overnight before continuing to Ecaps in the morning. His reasoning was sound, considering the significant distance remaining and the possibility of encountering Unknowns patrolling this area.

After setting up camp, we prepared a small meal before retiring. That night, I could not fall asleep, gazing into the stars above, wondering which was my star, my home planet, Earth, and if anyone was missing me.

We slept longer than anticipated, awakening to the sound of voices nearby. It was a relief to look around and recognize some friendly faces of the Ecaps harvesters greeting us.

Seeing us camped here undoubtedly surprised them, and by their muted murmur, it was evident that etched on Jonfrei's face was something of more than concern, easily uncharacteristic of his perceived nature.

Jonfrei discussed finding his dying father and his remains secure on the mountain, awaiting transport to Ecaps for burial. These harvesters opted to accompany us as we broke camp, with them having encountered some Unknowns earlier in the morning.

Upon our arrival at Ecaps, it was evident that word of Roulen's death had preceded our return, as many of Jonfrei's friends and family greeted us At Fate-Keepers Lodge; Enosewi and the elders had assembled upon learning Roulen had died on the mountain.

Enosewi, the shamanic priest Yurmond, and most Elders assembled, dispatching a recovery party to return to Gate-Keepers Mountain to retrieve Roulen's remains for a traditional water burial in the Ecaps River.

Pati'na came through the main door, sobbing, wanting to find me, "Thank you, Kenja."

Thank you. I looked at Pati'na puzzledly, not knowing what or why she might be thanking me.

"Jonfrei told us what you did by assisting his father Roulen in preparing for his death, guiding and comforting him during his final journey, sensing you had been chosen as Ecaps' Gatekeeper, Kenja,"

I tried to say 'no', definitely not, but I quickly was surrounded by Pati'na's mother, Yada, and her father, Sawecno. Soon arriving was Yerlaw, the Ecaps Defender, with everyone expressing grief upon learning of Jonfrei's father's death.

I silently watched the initial preparations for Roulen's 'Water Burial'. This ancient practice and tradition involves laying the deceased to rest in a crafted vessel that transports him along the flowing Ecaps River, where the sea waits to greet him.

I asked Pati'na more about this practice of water burials on Modeerf.

"Water represents our complete life cycle, Kenja, being created in the water of nature's womb and then emerging to live our lives. All rains, snow, and bodies of water eventually evaporate into the air. We believe that Roulen will also evaporate and then return from its gaseous state into a cloud to become rain again, completing the cycles of birth, death, and rebirth. As water gives life, it returns it to the Mordeef after death. Before his body is laid to rest in the Ecaps River, Roulen's body will be displayed in the Ancestor's Chamber, where Yurmond, our shamanic priest, will officiate."

I watched Paneta, the Medicinal Maker; prepare the Consecrated Anointing Water for the 'Washing of Hands 'ceremony. Jonfrei and his family, one after the other, would complete the ritual of continually pouring Sacred Water over Roulen's hands until sunset, using Ecaps's anointed Water Urn.

I noticed how music, prayers, and dancing accompanied the day-long service. In the evening, people wore floral attire. They later scattered flowers upon the waters of the Ecaps River as the Metamorphosis Casket, carrying Roulen's remains, journeyed, joining the waters of the sea.

The beauty of the Blue Lotus was their sacred symbol of creation and rebirth, and it became part of their mourning ritual. Yurmond, the Shamanistic Priest, led the ceremonies as the Celebration of Life for Roulen began.

Before the evening service, I asked Pati'na if we could go somewhere more private to discuss Ecaps' need for a new Gatekeeper.

"Pati'na, in the past, I have accepted things here and back on Earth without understanding their need."

"The understanding always seems to become clear when and if ever it's needed."

"If I should remain here on Modeerf, I would be honored to accept the position of the Gatekeeper, Pati'na."

I watched as Pati'na's face started to show concern.

"You look a little pale, Kenja."

"I noticed you wincing, rubbing your chest again."

"Are you feeling okay?"

"One of the Cuffers bumped me pretty hard when we were swimming with them the other day, and I think I bruised something, Pati'na. I'll be fine, thanks."

"Let's join the others down by the river, Kenja, for the evening's water burial."

# Words of Wisdom

With the burial service completed and most people heading home, I, too, returned to my cocoon hammock out in the open night air. There was now little doubt in my mind that I had an ongoing issue concerning my reoccurring fatigue.

Similar to when I was still a young boy living with my grandparents; I became aware that something was void in my life: the love of a mother. This present sense of becoming overwhelmed by perceived significant issues is one I must silently turn aside.

If only my grandmother were here to escort me around the back to her small workshop, where I would reveal my inner thoughts or concerns on canvas. I so clearly remember these were the only words spoken.

"Don't think, Kenja, Paint."

Looking back today, 'Don't think, Paint', what infinite wisdom these few words brought me my entire life. Whenever anxiety entered my life, I would reflect on this moment that happened so many years ago in a remote area in a small village in a workshop studio behind my grandmother's home.

After a few hours, Grandfather would return to Grandmother Dawnlilly's studio with his fishing pole and stand in the doorway. Grandfather, too, spoke no words. He stood there momentarily as if he had come to a fork in his path, waiting to see from which direction I would emerge.

How lucky is this? How many stars had to align for me to be at that exact place at that very moment with this authentic woman of wisdom, my Grandmother Dawnlilly?

I looked up to the night sky and couldn't find the answer. Maybe there truly is no answer. Then perhaps I should stop asking questions I already know have no definitive answers. These led only to more questions, leading to my anxiety in school and fear so much that the teacher would call on me to answer her questions about whatever. At this precise moment in the classroom, I always wished to become invisible and blend in with the background.

On Modeerf, incredible things happen constantly that you wouldn't think were possible. Every day, people are achieving things that I once considered impossible. It's where even the most unusual things don't seem unordinary. Even a horse with no legs wouldn't make people do a double-take. It's a world where anything can happen!

Then, in Heaven's name, why would I ever want to or even consider returning home to Earth? Why would I want to leave Modeerf? It's a fair enough question, but I don't have the answer, not now, at least.

Then I imagined being an answer, an answer to a question never asked. How many people unknowingly live their entire lives in this paradox of being born with a talent no longer of value today with the shifting sands of time?

Often, while listening to friends while sitting around the campfire, we would speak of our potential futures, sometimes our wants and wishes, and some would oddly have demands made of their future like it was under their control or something. These friends would undoubtedly be in for a shock later on in their lives with this mindset. Don't think, paint. Once more came thundering through the darkness to me.

I'll never forget Gloria, Little Fawn, saying, "If you want to make God laugh, just make a plan."

That, for me, summed things up.

Others expressed things that confused me when they first said them, like their desire to find themselves or where they truly belong. My interpretation is that they don't like what they see in their reflection or that they've been captivated by the romantic facet of an unreachable achievement. Don't think, paint, once more came thundering through the darkness to me.

The decision is near at hand, but not necessarily my hands. This ultimate decision of my life is to either stay on Modeerf or return to my beloved Earth. Either way, it's looking painful. Lately, I often see bursts of energy darting toward me. As they zoom by, they momentarily take on the fascial features of my Grandfather WiKenja.

Why is this happening? Things don't often happen here without reason. Perhaps this is a good time to remain alone and paint.

The canvas reveals an older man with a fishing pole heading to a bridge to fish. He looks content with his sauntering steps along the old dirt road. He never reached the bridge he was seeking, as the paint showed an old car traveling along this same old dirt road, rumbling toward the old fisherman from the opposite direction, heading to the old fishing bridge.

That older man, my grandfather, seems oblivious to the impending peril to soon intersect with his plans. As the old car heads directly toward my grandfather, knowing I must paint an obstacle to intercept the inevitable, my brush is dry and void of paint.

I'm hoping for the proper intervention as I now stand here wondering why this canvas appeared in the first place. These episodes never happened without cause, a means of forewarning, not giving the ability to acquit nor prevent, but to expose impending dangers to anyone with their receptors scanning the skies at this very moment.

"You look to be deep in thought, Kenja."

"Are you feeling any better?"

"Hi, Pati'na, yes, thanks."

I answered as I rose from resting, with that nagging chest pain persisting.

"How is Jonfrei doing?"

"How are you doing, Pati'na?"

Pati'na seemed to notice my effort in standing and suggested that after eating something, it would be best to rest some more before we went and checked on Jonfrei before retiring for the evening.

"Have you thought more about becoming our Gatekeeper, Kenja?"

This question brought me back to those youthful days, sitting around a campfire with my friends when someone suggested they wanted to find themselves or where they truly belonged. Recently, these topics have taken on a new meaning and perspective with everything happening in my existence.

Where's Teddy when you need him with his straightforward surgical way of dissecting issues? By this time, he would have easily made the proper decision and moved on. He always made it look so easy, even when others were panicking.

This situation of needing to make decisions brought me back to the day when the shocking outcome of my split-second decision forever changed everything related to risk.

It was a cool, crisp fall morning when I headed for the arena again. The roads were now dry after last night's rain. As I approached an intersection, the traffic light turned yellow right at that moment, where you can brake quickly or drive on, hoping it's a long yellow light.

I often ran late, once more behind schedule for a meeting or obligation. I hoped it was one of those long yellow lights I could beat, but not today. Somehow, today, I opted to brake hard, stopping up short.

Even though the car beside me was farther from the intersection than I was, it tried to beat the red light. The impending collision was a horrifying and sickening sound of metal, glass, airborne scrap car parts, and other debris exploding into an inferno, pieces flying everywhere. I ran toward this debris field, hoping to assist the injured in any way possible until help could arrive. But all those involved in the accident had perished, never having escaped the vehicles. This scene remains deeply etched in my mind.

I reflect on this split-second decision-making moment, wondering if my decision to jam on my brakes, did it keep me in my proper place and time or had placed me in the wrong place and time for the rest of my life.

Again, I could foresee that my subsequent decision here on Modeerf would bring me to that hypothetical yellow light.

I have no apparent reason to doubt that the images appearing on my canvas are a sign, an omen from one or both of my grandparents. There is, with certainty, a matter that needs my attention connected to my grandfather's well-being.

An ear-splitting crack of lightning suddenly accompanied a familiar roar of thunder; hearing my grandmother's words of wisdom, 'Don't think, Kenja. Paint'.

# The Power of Thought

After various adventures and misadventures here on Modeerf, and most recently, experiencing sadness related to the death of Roulen, Ecaps' Gatekeeper, it was a very moving experience to witness his 'Water Burial'. Having some downtime now has allowed me to reflect on what has happened during my journey.

With life here returning to normal, at least within the confines of Ecaps, I joined the others in performing the daily chores and necessary maintenance around the village. Not in an attempt to belong or fit in but to observe at arm's length the coming and going that flowed in a network of coordination and cooperation.

Pati'na noticed her mother, Yada, speaking with her best friend, Jonfrei, Ecaps' Pathfinder. The people of Ecaps often ask him if their journey would be safe. Pati'na then motioned to Kenja to join them.

After greeting Jonfrei, as expected, Pati'na asked if he could envision a safe passage for us if we visited the Tignish area later today. After some quick thought, Jonfrei advised,

"The Tignish tree continually requires caution at the best of times, far from settled times. You can be sure that, at minimum, an Unknowns scouting party will pass through the Tignish area, but my perception is just that: be cautious."

Attentiveness was always paramount in the area surrounding Tignish, which the Unknowns claimed as their inherited right and entitlement. Tignish was intended to be shared mutually among all the people of Modeerf.

"Would you like to visit Tignish today, Kenja?"

Pati'na's beaming expression again seemed to project what lay ahead, making me even more anxious than ever to explore and enjoy this Tignish opportunity, leaving us to experience whatever came our way.

Exploring the incredible landscapes while following this meandering path to Tignish, each bend was more wondrous than the previous and certainly was time well spent. Again, I'm still unsure about 'time' on Modeerf.

With her face glowing, Pati'na teasingly said:

"Wait until we reach the Tignish area, Kenja, because it is 'mad', Kenja. It's simply mad."

Pati'na wasn't exaggerating. This entire Tignish tract of land and countryside was unimaginable, easily separating itself beyond any valid visual description. I couldn't wait to see what might appear next, and, yes, this was mad.

As we neared the fabled Tignish tree, Pati'na must have read my mind, suggesting I wear a blindfold until we round the next few bends in the trail.

"Once we pass the final turn, the giant Tignish tree will stand before us, making its appearance, Kenja."

I could feel her excitement building as she took my hand and led me along the trail to this Tignish marvel.

"Making an appearance, Pati'na, really?"

"You might be building my expectations beyond any possible 'awe' moment."

With Pati'na's 'Wow', it wasn't hard to tell we had arrived at our destination.

"Here it is, Kenja, the Tignish tree."

Pati'na removed my blindfold, revealing a sight I had never experienced before nor contemplated in my wild imagination. Never could even my dream reveal more majesty than this, than this 'awe' moment.

"Wow, wow, wow."

These were the only words I could think of. Nothing could possibly prepare you for something like this unfolding before me. Affectionately squeezing Pati'na, whispering in her ear, "This is 'mad', Pati'na."

"This is so crazy, insanely, mad!"

This tree, this unbelievable tree, was the Mother-Load of mad. The size of this Tignish tree easily dwarfed the giant Sequoia trees of California. Even the infamous General Sherman would take a backseat to this Tignish tree.

This tree alone gave nature an entirely new definition, a perspective unequaled anywhere on Earth. Without the slightest exaggeration, no description would ever adequately describe this phenomenon. Calling it a tree in itself was an injustice.

Standing at its base was reminiscent of sailing the high seas. With its firmly affixed roots, the tree constantly swayed the terrain, the land being its cradle. The depth of its root system must be a world unto itself. Along with its moaning and groaning, I sensed its ability to breathe and purify a tremendous air volume. There was no wind to speak of, but this didn't prevent a deep howling from escaping the massive Upper Area, the crown of this jewel, and by doing so, dominating the visible distance with its superiority.

Having tended my little grove of Spruce saplings, the ones I planted with my grandfather years ago back in Witchenbrook, I had a reasonable concept of the volume of water required to nourish them for survival. This mad Tignish tree would undoubtedly require a small ocean of fresh water almost daily.

*I'll have to return to the Tignish tree with my sketchbook and make a detailed drawing of this 'mad' tree for my grandfather, for even he would be astonished by its size and capability of surviving for all eternity.*

Today's lesson for my grandfather would have to be; *Never say never until you've experienced the Tignish tree.*

I met up with Pati'na while she explored beneath the roots, some of which were the size of a regular-sized tree. It was truly unique to witness the giant of giants and see how it grew and survived with such massive roots firmly attached to the rocky crag, almost as if it had consumed the entire mountain. I was in awe of its scarred and weather-beaten agility and resilience.

This root system was massive and intriguing. I remember running through an immense corn maze when we were kids, exploring but never knowing exactly where we were. Yet, here in this open, unobstructed root system, it was uncanny how often Pati'na managed to hide from my view.

"Okay, I give up. Where are you this time, Pati'na?"

She appeared right in front of me, where a moment ago, I only saw tree roots. Then she disappeared and reappeared again, laughing.

"How are you doing that, Pati'na?"

"Doing what? You're teasing me again. Kenja, aren't you."

"I only wish I was teasing you, Pati'na."

"Seriously, how you seem to disappear from my view. How can that be possible?"

"I don't disappear, Kenja. I change colors."

"You say it like it is as natural as breathing, a normal thing."

Pati'na spun around, holding her finger to her lips.

"Quiet Kenja, listen."

Then she turned, pointing to an ascending root.

"Quickly, we must climb up and beyond this root system right now."

The anxiety etched on Pati'na's face was alarming in itself. Now scurrying through the massive intertwining root system, we silently arrived at a lush valley with a pond surrounded by mintberry ferns and other marsh-like vegetation.

There is now acuteness to Pati'na's behavior, becoming attentive to her surroundings. I assumed she was carefully turning mintberry ferns over, looking for any exposed glowing gray matter indicating the presence of the Unknowns. She turned to me, whispering:

"The Unknowns are in this area, close by, judging by the intensity of the gray glow of these mintberry ferns, Kenja."

"We can't let them find us or even know that we were anywhere near their sacred Tignish tree."

Pointing to the vegetation we were standing among;

"Quickly blend into these surrounding bigger ferns and flowers."

"Change your color now, Kenja."

"What?"

"Kenja, change your color!"

"What are you talking about? Change my color?"

"And how am I supposed to do that, Pati'na?"

"Quickly, Kenja, change now!"

"How?"

Now pleading with me, showing signs of frustration and anxiety.

"Kenja, talk to your body."

"You're not making any sense to me, Pati'na."

"Tell it of your need to survive, Kenja. Which requires it to change your color and right now!"

The snap of a branch had me turning to see Unknowns advancing. Panic filled my entire being, begging me to opt for flight or fight. But my grandfather's vision brought the request to remain and blend in.

Amazingly, the Unknowns looked at the pond and surrounding area, right at Pati'na, and then, terrifyingly, directly at me. Then, turned around, conveying to the other Unknowns that no one was at Tignish Pond.

Maybe the Unknown didn't notice me, but how could he not have heard my heart pounding while trying to jump out of my chest?

"We're safe now, Kenja."

I just stood there, still frozen to the spot.

"Let's move on."

Feeling unsteady and exhausted, I needed to rest without causing alarm, but my mind was sounding alarm bells while trying to catch my breath.

After all, my entire coaching staff and I completed our quarterly physical only two weeks before the start of this journey. Just the same, I'll have Kenny arrange an appointment with Doc as soon as I return, provided I do return.

"Wait, I'll need time to steady my nerves and pull myself together, Pati'na; too much just happened."

"You did well, Kenja."

I certainly didn't think I did well at all. I froze, expecting to die at any moment. I'm sure my so-called colors were 'white as a ghost'.

"Your colors were amazing, blending in perfectly."

Pati'na, now taking me by the shoulders and turning me to face her, congratulated me.

"You were teasing me all along, right?"

I wasn't teasing her, but I was surely kidding myself about there not being an issue with this nagging pain that would need some attention soon.

As we continued walking, without getting into too much detail about how being one color or another on Earth had a huge influence on the availability of so many options and your potential, I managed to get Pati'na to understand that being able to change color is not an option and never will be an option on Earth.

As I was walking and lost in thought, preoccupied with what had just taken place, I wondered how changing the color of our skin on Earth could potentially solve many of the racial issues we face today. Why does the color of our skin impact our lives when, fundamentally, we are all the same?

Hearing a shrill voice filled with 'panic', I snapped back to reality.

"Watch out, Kenja!"

Looking up too late, I could not stop my forward motion; I fell into an abyss with Pati'na frantically urging me to fly. Panicking, I spread my arms as my descent speed increased, still desperately trying to fly again.

I severed my hand when impacting my wrist on a razor-sharp edge. Going into shock camouflaged this excruciating pain. I felt terror and panic and continued plummeting like a rock, with my speed increasing until Pati'na managed to deflect my path of descent enough to slam us into a protruding ledge.

Once again, resulting from this shock, I lost connection with my grandfather's teachings and began to panic, really freaking out, fearing the worst. Pati'na applied pressure to my wrist, and the bleeding slowed, giving me at least some hope of survival.

"Okay, Kenja, you must focus now, using only positive intentions."

"Tell me you understand. Kenja, stay with me here. Tell me you understand."

I looked at my handless arm, and the anxiety on Pati'na's face yelled out.

"I don't understand anything happening here now or ever before!"

"How are we ever going to get out of here, Pati'na? I'm going to die here?"

"Kenja, you once told me that back on Earth, you accepted things without fully understanding the reason and that the understanding will reveal itself if and when needed. This moment will be your moment of truth."

"Ya, well, Pati'na, I'm not back on Earth, am I?"

"Kenja, you'll have to grow a new wrist and hand soon."

"You're 'mad', Pati'na, and not the sane, fuzzy, attractive kind! You're just frigging insanely mad!"

"Well, at least me being 'mad' is a good sign of your focus returning."

She firmly grabbed Kenja's shoulders and shook him. "Okay, Kenja, is there anyone on Earth that can regenerate limbs?"

"No, Pati'na, that's crazy."

"No human can regenerate anything."

"Yes, organs like a kidney or a heart can be transplanted."

*What is she doing? This can't be happening now or during all of this exposure. I have to get away from her and her inane questions.*

"None of this is helping me, Pati'na, so unless you can give me a transplant, I have a serious problem here."

"Think hard, stay focused, Kenja, and calm yourself."

"I'm right here with you and won't let you give up."

"Think one more time about regeneration."

"No, no, no!"

"You are so stubborn, Pati'na!"

"No, it's not possible!"

"What about other species, Kenja?"

"Are there any capable of regenerating limbs?"

"A salamander can regenerate a limb, but it takes six months."

I have to find a way to get up and at least try to climb up out of this fissure. Anything but these relentless, useless questions.

"Look…can you help me instead of asking these stupid questions?"

"Listen to me, listen, Kenja."

"I am trying to help you; I am desperately trying to help you."

"Are there any other examples, Kenja?"

"An octopus and some cuttlefish can regenerate severed tentacles."

"So, what makes you think you cannot do this?"

"So, Pati'na, that's the plan. What the hell are you suggesting?"

Pati'na cut me off in half-sentence,

"Give your body permission to heal and release your body's regenerative powers, like a loyal dog waiting for your attention."

"If you don't release your body's powers, it will remain by your side like an obedient dog until you unleash it and find the solution to your problem."

When life got too stressful when I was young, I often felt the urge to shut everything down and hide under my blankets, hoping that things would disappear when I woke up or crawled out from under the covers. That never happened then, and it's probably not going to happen now.

Looking at my arm, now devoid of a hand, I know I'm in trouble. Not even Grandfather spoke of regenerating limbs. I know I have to keep my panic at bay, or as Pati'na believes, there is no tomorrow.

"Kenja, please focus and try to remember if you've ever been able to use your mind to change something by directing your body to do so,"

"I have tinnitus, and I don't think it's relevant, Pati'na."

"Please explain what tinnitus is, Kenja, and let me determine its significance,"

"Tinnitus is a persistent noise inside your head that you cannot escape, like air hissing from a hose or a marching band parading loudly between your ears. Occasionally, I can talk this noise into shutting down when trying to sleep. It doesn't stop immediately, but soon, it will slowly fade to an inaudible murmur I can tolerate."

"That's exactly what I've been looking for, Kenja."

"You can do this, stay with me, Kenja, stay with me."

I now sense losing contact, feeling things changing as the shock wears off, and an awareness of an unendurable pain sets into my doomed reality.

"Kenja, stay awake!"

"Listen to my voice!"

"I think I found the solution to our dilemma."

Sensing she was losing him, Pati'na started shaking Kenja violently.

"Wake up, wake up, Kenja, listen!"

"I found some remnants of dry-water in my satchel."

"I will let the dry-water bead drip onto the severed area of your arm. But it doesn't work if you are projecting negative thoughts. You must convey positive thoughts of energies while releasing your body to go and fix it, go and fix it, using your healing powers, your distinct dry-water, Kenja."

I could feel the energy to resist draining from my body and the will to survive quickly fading. In desperation, I became aware of an evil presence in my mind urging me to walk back toward the edge of the ledge, enter the door to eternal infinity, and step away and end it all.

The battle between Pati'na's words for survival and Kenja's demons was relentless, but fatigue concluded with Pati'na's words of wisdom, hope, and survival prevailing.

Her voice alone formed audible words, the words needed to draw Kenja away from the inviting edge of this steep ledge, the one his next step could lead to a pain-free infinite eternity.

At this very moment, he was so worn and tired that everything worth fighting for had become insignificant.

Kenja only longs to surrender and then, through eternity, return to Celeste, his soulmate, Grandfather WiKenja, and Brother Teddy. He needs to return home to be with them and me again.

"Kenja, I'm going to apply the bead of dry-water now."

"You are going to encounter some Slugmuck-like experiences."

"I'll meet you on the other side."

"You can do this, Kenja, because I see your truth."

# The Vortex and the Odyssey

Listening to Pati'na's fading voice, I suddenly found myself in ebony darkness, in the middle of a vast swirling tornado, pulling me in deeper and deeper. The vortex was so intense that it was impossible to keep focused as it spun faster and faster. I felt like I was being sucked into another world, and there was no way out.

The pounding noise and jarring pressure were so intense it felt like my bones would shatter, disintegrating to powder. Only to be ejected into a peaceful and calm place, which must be 'The Sea of Tranquility', often spoken of.

Describing this vastness full of unimaginable colors and dimensions would be as futile as attempting to define color to someone born blind. Even the giant Tignish tree would seem dwarfed in this kingdom.

Finding myself alone, I sensed a frighteningly void of any meaningful thought, totally abandoned by any and all senses, standing in the middle of all eternity, standing unsuspended, not by anything I could see.

As I regained my faculties, my eyes slowly focused on a slightly blurry sign, but then it became more in focus, 'Entrance' with an arrow pointing down a hallway. I felt a strong magnetic force pulling me toward the entrance as if an invisible force urged me to keep moving forward. I kept walking down the hallway and saw someone in the distance.

"Excuse me. I'm looking for the 'entrance' door. Would you know where it is?"

"Just go through those doors there."

"There are no doors there."

"Then don't go through them."

Becoming frustrated, as I turned to point out that there were no doors, someone walked out of the entrance door that wasn't there a second ago, saying,

"Be seated. Anthony and two doctors will meet you in the waiting area."

I see these two doctors in white coats; each seemingly uses a cane to get around.

One of them pointing and gesturing to me.

"Wear a 'Johnny Shirt' and lie on that hospital gurney; we'll be right with you."

This balding, handle-barred mustached cartoon-looking doctor checked my name tag, asking, "Are you Anthony?"

"Sometimes I'm Anthony, sometimes I'm called Kenja, it depends."

"Aha." He sounded like he had just caught someone with their fingers in the cookie jar.

"Only sometimes, he's Anthony, doctor, only sometimes."

He waved his cane around in the air, motioning his sarcastic astonishment.

"Only sometimes, Dr. Cane, only sometimes."

"He's going to fit in here just fine, isn't he, Dr. Cane?"

"He is, indeed, Dr. Cane."

"Wait, you are both Dr. Cane?"

"Whoa, he is a clever one, too, isn't he, Dr. Cane?"

"Yes indeed, Dr. Cane, but we're always in a hurry, right, Dr. Cane!"

"Yes, we're always in a hurry, Dr. Cane!"

"Hurry, hurry, hurry, that's us!"

"That's why they call us the Hurry-Canes."

"Hurricanes, do you get it? Aren't we a gas, Anthony?"

"We are the laughing gas for your operation."

Suddenly, a booming voice, a resounding one full of authority, enters the operating arena, bellowing.

"Hey! You two again."

"What are you two doing in here?"

Looking at me, asking, "Do you know who these two are?"

"They said they were my anesthesiologists."

"Anesthesiologists, they are the custodians here, Anthony."

Hurriedly turning to chase both Dr. Canes, "You're custodians, you damn fools, not comedians, custodians."

"They keep cutting the heads off the mop and using them as canes."

Assisting this booming voice, a porter started wheeling me into a surgical area with various procedures indicated on the adjacent doors.

We were entering a zone with sections for each of the eight planets. As we went into the Earth section, there was a considerably sized department called 'Questions Manufacturing Sector', where questions were produced nonstop, 24/7. Nearby, I saw a small auditorium called 'Department of Answers', where answers were provided during a typical five-day work week from 9 a.m. to 5 p.m.

Awareness of this discrepancy alone answered many questions; once again, I was aware enough to realize we were going into the wrong procedure section as they were taking me to the 'heart transplant' operating theater.

"Whoa, there's been a mistake here. I am here for a new hand, not a transplant of any organ, let alone a heart transplant."

The porter checked my identification wristband.

"It appears we have a 'Kenja' here today, and he is indeed here for a new hand."

"Well, let's get him that new hand. Which one is missing?"

"It looks like it's the left one missing,"

"Well, let's start there, a new hand it will be."

And off they wheeled me past all the transplant operation theaters and into the 'Limb Replacement' section.

I met with the actual anesthesiologist, Dr. Putuout, and she did just that.

After being given general anesthesia, I had some really vivid and wild dreams. They were so unusual that I'm unsure how to describe them anymore. My perception of what's weird or strange has completely changed since I spent time in this alternate reality called Modeerf.

With my new hand, I shook hands with the doctors for helping me as they led me to another area of this seemingly endless complex.

I entered a doorway with a sign indicating the department for assembling 'forks-in-the-roads', where they were seemingly being created like they were going out of style.

This assembly line looks like a modern version of an old railway yard with all those track switchers, producing direction options in every imaginable direction.

Not totally unexpected the 'Return to Earth' door was closed: 'Temporarily Out Of Order; Closed for Maintenance'.

At this point, taking the exit to Modeerf was still an option, but the one with the big question mark on the door was the most intriguing one for me.

I remember my grandfather telling me, 'that there was no such thing as a stupid question asked. It's only stupid if this question is never asked'.

As I opened the door with a question mark on it, I found myself in a strange and fascinating place. Many wise people from history, like Solomon, Albert Einstein, and Isaac Newton, sat together in a room resembling an ancient Roman Senate. They were wearing robes and seemed very important. The room was filled with floating numbers and equations that looked like they were dancing in space, sensing many mysteries waiting to be solved in that room.

As I gazed out into the distance, I noticed a group of bright lights, one of which quickly approached me and turned into the familiar form of my mother, Dawn. Even though the image only lasted for a moment, it made me think that when we pass away, our loved ones who have already passed might be there to greet us in the afterlife.

As I climbed the broad steps of the meandering staircase, an imposing figure veiled in vapor stood at the top, beckoning me through the dissipating mist.

We were again ascending to another vast, bright, colorful, multi-dimensional area outside the Senate. This holographic imagery told me this was the opportunity to ask my questions, those that never seemed to have an answer.

As quickly as I posed these questions, crystal-clear, concise answers came.

"Why are we on Earth?"

"To experience love."

"Why do some people struggle to meet their basic needs and live in poverty, while others seem to have everything they need and more without any effort?"

"You choose your experiences during conception."

"Why do some of us live for a few days and others 100 years?"

"There is no such thing as time in the universe, and on Earth, humans are the only ones who use instruments to measure something that doesn't exist."

"Why do good and evil people exist, and why are even the deplorable people loved?"

"On Earth, positive and negative energies attract similar energies. These energies exist in physical forms and interact with the world around us."

"Why do we fall in love with some people and not others?"

"Again, the energy forces that we inherit are the energy we are attracted to."

"Why are there Lesbians and homosexuals?"

"Earth is the only station where both genders exist."

"Sometimes people emit a certain kind of energy that can be more attractive than their physical appearance as we typically see it."

"There are times when a person's energy or vibe can be more appealing than their outer appearance, which we usually notice at first glance."

I asked question after question, receiving answers I understood and readily accepted. But now I questioned the intent of gaining these understandings.

"Can I reveal these insights?"

"I'm eagerly waiting for a reply. This question is important because if I don't get an answer, others might think that my cognitive abilities have been sorely compromised during this transition."

"Listen, I don't understand what I'm supposed to do with this intellectual information."

A big booming, vibrating voice replied, "That's right, you don't."

This unimposing white-robed energy field told me to prepare myself for the re-enter into my body, one I will find being complete again.

As I entered my body, I felt physical and psychological characteristics uniting with the continuous transfer of acceptance and rejection from my altered state. I could feel the constant struggle and resettling taking place.

Finally, the struggle ebbed, and once more, I groggily awakened, finding myself sheltered safely in my cocoon hammock back in Ecaps with cold shivers running down my spine. There was so much to try to understand or not.

"Welcome home, my two-handed Kenja."

Looking down at my hand, I realized that I was whole again, but in more ways than one.

"Did you learn any lessons during your journey, Kenja?"

"I did, Pati'na. Many would be more than beneficial to return to earth with. But you won't need any of them here on Modeerf, Pati'na."

But I could easily envision my grandfather becoming fascinated that I might obtain unimaginable insights in one lesson.

# The Futile Exercise

Contemplating my past, my home, and even Earth on this new day, focusing on my existence, one I was beginning to question honestly. Is it possible that Modeerf is the real world and Earth is merely a fantasy?

Throughout my life, I have often postponed tasks for another day, at times two, leaving many things undone. However, Pati'na's belief that there is no tomorrow, only today, makes me question the significance of my procrastination.

"You look deep in thought, Kenja. Am I interrupting?"

"No. No, come on in. Seeing you on such a glorious morning makes it that much nicer."

"Do you, or should I say we, have any plans for the day, Pati'na?"

Kenja stands while greeting Pati'na as she enters, sitting at his kitchen table.

"I was hoping today might be a good day for you to tell me more of your Earth, Kenja. I don't know much about your Earth besides what you told me the day we met the little people. Remember the Glimps? Wasn't that a day to remember?"

"That was such a fun, magical day, and sharing this encounter with you while experiencing their precious little world was awesome, Pati'na."

"So, Kenja, would today be a good day for you to help me learn more about where you came from, your Earth?"

"Come from Pati'na, it's come from. Came from could indicate I do not intend on returning."

There was an awkward silence between us with this unexpected interpretation. I was desperately torn between my future and the untold treasures and mysterious connections available here with Pati'na on Modeerf versus returning home to my life on Earth. This omni-silence confirmed that I wasn't alone in these thoughts.

"All right, my inquisitive Miss Pati'na, the Earth it will be."

Kenja put the kettle on, preparing to make tea as they continued their conversation.

"Earth truly is a wonderful place, Pati'na. It, too, is quite an amazing evolution. Being one of many planets in the Milky Way Galaxy, which, I think, is one of the estimated 100 to 200 billion assumed Galaxies in the Universe."

"We have a sun that produces light and heat, similar to your dry-water here on Modeerf."

Pati'na nearly choked and spat out her tea.

"Wow, wait a minute, Kenja, you have a son who produces light and heat?"

"Whoa, Pati'na. No, I don't have a son. It's another kind of sun, not the one you're thinking of."

This conversation could become hilarious, confusing, or, more likely, both. Again, I heard my grandfather tell me, Kenja, words matter.

"Earth is a breathtakingly gorgeous planet, boasting an abundance of freshwater bodies of lakes, streams, and rivers. It has five oceans and three seas filled with saltwater, teeming with marine life."

Raising his arms to the ceiling, Kenja mimicked an imaginary mountain.

"The mountains are so tall that they appear to stretch, wanting to touch the sky. You can explore various environments, from vast, arid deserts to lush, abundant forests, each with unique flora and fauna. On top of that, our tropical humid rainforests are teeming with life."

Kenja checked for signs of interest from Pati'na, who was still listening intently.

"After billions of years of evolution, Earth has become the planet it is today. Like here, Pati'na, all life forms share a fundamental and vital purpose of survival, essential for life's reproduction development."

"It does sound beautiful, Kenja. It's easy to understand and appreciate your desire to return home to your Earth. I'm captivated by your descriptions."

"Please don't stop now, as I'm waiting for you to get to the mad part about you having a son."

Pati'na laughed and repositioned her chair. Her fingers combed through her long blond hair, and her eyes quickly revealed her deep, passionate feelings for Kenja.

"I'm truly into this, Kenja, so don't you even think about stopping now."

"Well, I'm sorry, but this might be where the beautiful part ends, Pati'na, as it might have taken billions of years in the making, but man has managed to destroy much of it exceedingly quicker."

Kenja rubbed his chin, contemplating whether to end things here, as the following words would easily not be very enticing, to say the least. But they would be honest and truthful.

"Unfortunately, throughout too much history, as the human population greatly increased, the interests of the world's strongest nations have often taken priority over the planet's overall well-being, particularly in recent times."

Kenja now noticed Pati'na's frown getting more pronounced; unsure, he cautiously continued, hesitatingly.

"Sadly, Pati'na, governments have implemented regulations and policies prioritizing the financial success of these nation's leaders, at the expense of the greater good, always resulting in economics trumping the environment."

That might have done it.

Pati'na was holding up her hand.

"Stop, Kenja."

"Well, you started by describing that your Earth is a beautiful place. It doesn't sound like it's wonderful at all anymore."

"Don't confuse Earth with humans, Pati'na. Earth itself is a wonderful planet, as is most of mankind. It's the greed and misunderstanding and the extent to which this greed has surpassed the ability of the Earth itself to cope. Eventually, Earth will make the necessary corrections by eliminating mankind, the process that is slowly killing her."

Kenja took Pati'na's cup, pouring more tea before continuing.

"Once more, Earth will prevail, becoming the motherland of survival; she will survive. On the other hand, the greed and abuse of human vanity will eventually destroy itself along with much of the animal and native kingdom with its blissful ignorance. Perhaps the next opportunity for human existence on Earth will not let history repeat itself."

"And you want to go back to your Earth, Kenja?"

I was not sure any longer. I was no longer as confident, but I didn't want to give any miscued signals to Pati'na, one I might regret later. But spending time here with Pati'na and the people of Ecaps and how they respect their plant, Modeerf, I'm no longer as sure as to what path I'll take when I do reach that fork in the road.

"Kenja, what do you mean by a million or billions of years, and what exactly is time?"

Kenja displays a deep sense of relief that their topic of conversation has shifted.

"Time, Pati'na would undoubtedly be the biggest difference between Earth and Modeerf."

While trying to impress by bolstering his knowingly false display of knowledge, Kenja reverts to his clouded memory of his school days, almost robotically formulating words.

"In simple terms, Earth revolves around the sun while rotating on its axis. It takes one day for the Earth to complete one rotation on its axis, and 365 rotations to complete one full orbit around the sun, which we call a year…”

Uncontrollably, Pati’na blurted out, “I think you lost me around the mad part about you having a son again, Kenja.”

As suspected, this conversation becoming hilarious or confusing was now evident. Then again, if I decide to remain here on Modeerf with Pati’na and the others from Ecaps, there will be plenty of time to come to recount and give some form of definition to all of Earth’s qualities, perhaps former ones, but qualities just the same.

“I think trying to relate the concept of time we acknowledge on Earth would be a more interesting and easier topic for me, Pati’na.”

“Okay, ‘time’ it is, Kenja from Earth.”

“You are just too cute for your good, Miss Pati’na.”

If my brother Teddy were here, he could describe this interpretation of time in a few concise words. I’m sure my explanation will be long-winded, baffling, and half-witted, leaving Pati’na more confused.

“I remember this quote that I had to memorize for Mr. Murray’s science class, Pati’na. We measure the continuing succession from the past through the present into the future by time. Does this make any sense to you?”

“Not really, Kenja, and even if it did, I wouldn’t admit to it.”

“But I benefit from spending time with you and am amused by how your demeanor and attitude change when you get serious about telling me something. I’d rather you tell me in your own everyday words, Kenja.”

Kenja displayed a much-needed sigh of relief.

“Oh man, Pati’na, how vainly stupid I’ve been trying to be something other than myself, the real me.”

“I think the real you is the real deal, Kenja.”

“You are more of a person than you could ever imagine, and I hope you will find the chance to return to your special place, your Earth.”

An awkward silence filled the air for a few moments, trying to find a means of returning to the intent of our conversation. Hesitating, Kenja added.

"Time has become our nemesis on Earth, Pati'na, attaching itself to everything imaginable. From daytime to nighttime, one time, some time, any time, the list keeps going on. We have the first time, the last time, the only time, the springtime, the best to the worst of times."

Kenja pauses, relaxing, becoming more comfortable.

"Time. It's always there, 24 hours a day, every single day, everywhere; time is always in your face."

Kenja watched carefully for any sign that Pati'na might be making sense of what he was trying to convey despite his muddled explanation.

"Okay, Kenja, I think I'm getting the picture."

Considering my inapt explanation, this should be good.

"Then, I would assume time became the Earth's Ruler, with Earthlings becoming its slaves."

With a big smirk on his face, Kenja laughs. Having difficulty disputing Pati'na's analysis, he decided this would have to do, no pun intended, for the time being.

"Well, that's not exactly what I was going to say, but thinking about it from your perspective, I can appreciate your conclusion, Pati'na."

"You are fortunate, Pati'na, not to have any measurable time here on Modeerf."

"Often, you seem to be talking in riddles, Kenja."

"Or should I be saying, 'sometimes'?"

"Pati'na, the more I think about how I can convey the meaning of time to you, the more I realize I don't have the time," causing both Pati'na and Kenja to burst into spontaneous laughter.

"Okay, Kenja, other than love then, tell me what you think are the best and the worst things you have on your Earth."

"That would be so much easier."

"As you said, the whole meaning of life on Earth, Pati'na, is the existence of love and to experience love, so elusive for some, so negative for others, and so devastatingly filled with heartbreak when it ends."

Taking a much exaggerated tongue-in-cheek sarcastic bow, Kenja continued.

"So, without overthinking the answers to your questions, I would say that other than love, here, in my humble opinion, are the best and the worst things about living on Earth."

Wanting to get this right, Kenja opted to pause momentarily before continuing;

"Let's start with the worst. The worst thing for me would be the innovation of time because, as I've said, we keep wasting it and chasing it, leaving us somewhat captive to it."

"Time is a powerful force that rules our lives on Earth. We often check the time not because we want to know what time it is, but because we hope to see what time it isn't, that it's not too late or too early for something. In the past, we measured time by the day, which was much easier to deal with. But today, we measure time by tiny milli-seconds, which can be overwhelming, often escalating anxiety. Time has become like a harsh dictator that controls every aspect of our lives."

Taking another drink of tea while trying to rub this continuing irritation in his chest indiscreetly, Kenja smiles;

"Surely the best thing on Earth to me is the written word being on the opposite end of the spectrum from time. Once we put pen to paper, composing anything from a postcard to a scholarly tome, we leave a part of us behind, using this unique opportunity of the written word. Although I'm a spiritualist, not a religious person, if I should ever meet up with God one day, I would thank him for giving humanity the written word."

"The written word, Kenja, that's interesting. Why the written word?"

"I marvel at the thought that others could understand and interpret my little markings on a piece of paper, written words, even if read a thousand years from now, Pati'na. These little scribbles on paper could convey my message to future generations. That fascinates me in such a positive way by me leaving a record behind rather than a footprint."

"I appreciate your insight, Kenja. It's a great perspective that has given me a new understanding. Thank you for sharing it with me."

Pati'na stood, stretching her long, stiff legs before continuing. Kenja again marvels at the sheer beauty of her physical shape.

"I appreciate you taking the time to talk with me about this, Kenja. It's nice to share our interests." I got the impression that class had ended for the day as Pati'na started pirouetting, indicating she had decided it was now time just to let loose and have some fun, tripping the light fandango, rejoicing in her ecstasy, and all of the other clichés available while freely dancing all around, teasingly provoking a response from me, exhibiting her own 'Joie de Vivre', singing out, "Tell me again about your mad son, Kenja, from Earth," as Pati'na stood and teasingly started running around to the opposite side of the table.

"This son of yours sounds 'mad, Kenja, super mad', just like you, my adorable, sweet Kenja."

Pati'na fluttered toward me like a carefree butterfly, then darted again outdoors, leaving me with barely a glimpse of her form as, like a butterfly, she went from flower to flower, playing and laughing as carefree as a bird.

I chased her through this seemingly never-ending field of flowers, hopes, and dreams.

As I reached out to her, Pati'na stumbled and fell into a bed of flowers. In my attempt to avoid her, I, too, lost my balance and landed on top of her.

"What do you want to talk about now, my Kenja from Earth?"

I'm sure that I heard her say, "My."

# The Chance Encounter

Maintaining a balance in life is crucial for all living things on Modeerf, including the bog beetle and the mintberry tree. Sadly, the bog beetle's infestation has steadily declined the cultivation and natural processes necessary for these vital berries. This scarcity has threatened the Unknowns community's existence and caused chaos and conflict with no viable alternative to replacing the missing properties, causing the citizens to lose faith in Hannah and her leadership.

The situation has become so dire that the community's survival depends on the Unknowns' leadership breaking the boundary agreements that had long existed with Ecaps. This has resulted in Vexiana, along with every other member of the Unknowns, having to venture deeper into the recognized Ecaps territory.

While focusing entirely on her search for the Mintberries, becoming oblivious to her immediate surroundings, she only noticed people nearby when it was too late; they called out to her, "Hey, Pati'na, come join us."

"We're heading home to Ecaps, too."

Pati'na? They called me Pati'na?

Fully aware that she was trespassing, Vexiana momentarily experienced panic and fear. Still, she tried to remain composed, as she had no other clear option.

"Oh, hi, thanks."

"Wait up, and I'll join you."

Vexiana, still unsure, approached these young women from Ecaps, searching for any sign they may have realized their mistake in speaking with whom they perceived to be Pati'na.

"What are your plans with Kenja for the rest of the day, Pati'na?"

So, that is who Hannah had seen Pati'na with while walking her horse with no legs.

As Vexiana walked into the community center, she spotted Jonfrei, an old childhood friend who was now a leader in the community. Vexiana was trying to hide her true identity because she wanted to continue to masquerade as Pati'na and blend in with the Ecaps community. Meeting Jonfrei face-to-face would be a crucial test for this eventual masquerade.

"Hi, Pati'na. Yerlaw asked me if I happened to see you to be sure to mention that he had something urgent to discuss with you."

Vexiana thought to herself, *How amazing this was to be happening and by such a simple chance encounter.*

Vexiana knew that Yerlaw was the community defender who handled most of the strategic affairs for Ecaps, knowing that whatever he had to discuss, big or small, would undoubtedly be significant.

Entering the village, she searched for a secluded place to gather her thoughts. Yerlaw's urgent matter made Vexiana realize the possible value of this information to Hannah and the Unknowns, who would surely appreciate it.

With her untrustworthy, wobbly legs and frayed nerves, she had to dig deep to put forth her best effort to impersonate Pati'na since their childhood encounters. Hoping that her cousin Pati'na still exhibited the same qualities and traits Vexiana remembered, trying to imitate the more obvious ones, especially Pati'na's Joie de Vivre nature and exuberant enjoyment of life.

Walking toward her childhood friend Yerlaw, her heart racing, sensing the possibility, no more likely the probability, of this ruse heading south in a hurry.

Deciding to partially conceal her face with her hand to better the odds while trying to control her shaking knees, Vexiana spoke to Yerlaw as calmly as possible.

"Hi, Yerlaw. I met up with Jonfrei."

She constantly looked for any hint of needing to escape quickly.

"And he mentioned that you might want to speak with me."

"Hey, Pati'na, yeh, I wanted to remind you that you will need to get more dry-water as we seem to be running low much quicker than usual. It's not urgent or immediate, but sooner than later if you can."

Jonfrei motioned to Pati'na.

"Come closer; it looks like you have something in your eye. Let me take a look for you."

Even with this close-up look into her eyes, Yerlaw's body language did not hint at suspicion, not even a little.

By masquerading as Pati'na, Vexiana now realized the feasibility of this possible ruse. It was unquestionably not only filled with revenge but also with out-and-out spite.

Wanting to remove any doubt about the authenticity of this masquerade for Yerlaw, Vexiana decided it best to add Kenja's name to the charade.

"Yes, I'll ask Kenja to join me."

Luckily for Vexiana, by sheer coincidence, the first person she met mentioned this stranger, Kenja, a friend of Pati'na.

"Thanks, Pati'na. Sorry, I'm in a hurry. I'll see you later, and…Oh, and say 'Hi' to Kenja for me."

Tentatively walking along the path out of the village, Vexiana spotted Pati'na walking toward her with someone she assumed must be Kenja. Quick to dart under cover, remaining unnoticed, she waited for them to pass, fortunately, fully absorbed in conversation on their way to Ecaps.

Vexiana darted into the wooded area, scampering along a small brook, heading back to the Unknowns' compound in search of Hannah. She wanted to relate this opportunity to the information she had intercepted. Once again displaying her ability to think on the spot, Vexiana had already devised a plan, one manifested and conceived with revenge.

The Unknowns sentries sounded the alarm as they witnessed someone running with sheer terror, as though they were the terrified prey of the menacing flesh-eating Klongs that still inhabited the forests surrounding the Unknowns stockade. The guards seized the intruder only to realize it was Vexiana. Her display of confusion, impossible-to-understand intense emotions, desperately seeking Hannah's whereabouts.

They had now escorted Vexiana safely inside the compound, where she was calmed down enough to relate her recent experiences and wanted to speak with Hannah. Some of the female guards continued talking with Vexiana, assuring her that Hannah would return soon and having her comfortably rest where she remained anxiously waiting in Hannah's lodge.

The guards soon dispatched a runner to find Hannah, calling for more Centurions to watch over an exhausted Vexiana, guarding her safety and secret.

Knowing the whereabouts of Hannah, it wasn't long before Hannah received word of Vexiana's excited state of discovery, one she so desperately wanted to share with Hannah. Hannah knew that it would have to be something significant to provoke this current state of excitement in Vexiana, and she, too, could feel her excitement building as she was escorted back to the Unknowns' compound.

Entering the compound and seeing all of the extra security around Vexiana's quarters was one more sign of the assumed significance of Vexiana's urgency to meet with Hannah. Seeing the telltale signs of how tattered some of Vexiana's clothing appeared, her shins and forearms scraped and bleeding, which was evidence of her urgency to return to the Unknowns' compound.

Hannah called for some nursemaids, "Why hasn't anyone cleaned and dressed these wounds on Vexiana?"

“She was so exhausted, Hannah, we thought it best to allow her to rest. These were only superficial wounds.”

Hannah gently woke Vexiana, and the feasibility of gaining access to the dry-water was revealed.

Hannah cleared Vexiana’s room before allowing Vexiana to begin elaborating on the day’s events, knowing that whatever would cause such a desire to meet with her with such urgency had to be shielded for the time being.

Soon, the length of their meeting was causing a stir among the sentries, and some overheard comments soon spread throughout the compound that something unthought of was about to happen.

Hannah summoned the Governor and the Elders to Vexiana’s quarters, which added credibility to the day’s significance.

# The Plan

The Chief Sentry sounded the alarm as people continued to file into the Assembly Lodge, anticipating that something significant had occurred, or better yet, somebody had discovered an adequate supply of mintberry.

The chatter increased as people constantly filed in and began to take their seats, with the hall soon reaching near capacity.

Hannah called the meeting to order.

"Order. Order."

Hannah repeated herself, "Order. Please, will the remainder of those standing be seated?"

While seeming to have a sense of relief, an insight of rejuvenation, Hannah began, "Today marks the beginning of a new era."

Momentarily pausing, "At long last, the day has come when we can rid ourselves of our reliance on the existence of the mintberry's properties."

Jubilation and triumphant yells of euphoria overwhelmingly followed.

Hannah echoed, "Order, order."

Once Hannah restored order, she shared Vexiana's recent unplanned experience that led to an equally unintended exposure that Pati'na was the key to the dry-water. She then outlined the basics of a plan to regain control of the location of the dry-water.

Asked to address the assembled, Vexiana related her childhood experiences shared with Pati'na and how easily they could be mistaken for each other, which led to today's encounter in Ecaps. She then detailed how this encounter triggered a very feasible concept of deception, resulting in the kidnapping of Pati'na's horse, the one with no legs.

Hannah waited for the din to subside before continuing,

"To summarize."

She was, again, waiting to ensure people's full attention.

"At this time, the plan involves taking Pati'na's horse as collateral and exchanging it for information Pati'na possesses on accessing the dry-water. This may be our final opportunity for survival as the continuous destruction of the mintberry trees, berries, and their availability leaves us in a very precarious position."

Once more, Hannah looked around, assuring people's complete attention, before continuing.

"Our military personnel have proposed a plan to capture Eaus'eche by entering the compound and seizing the hostage. Our last team, which comprises the governors, the elders, and myself, is responsible for devising a deceptive strategy that requires precision and timing to guarantee that any practical chance of success will be recognized and included in our plan."

Hannah rose slowly; displaying her now revived confidence as being restored, and began, "The objective here is first to test the loyalty between Pati'na, either to that of her horse or to the citizens of Ecaps themselves. The only way to determine this outcome is to carry out the task."

Enosila, the Elder from the Upper Area, called for a 'point of personal privilege' on the matter. Hannah again sought control of the meeting amid the spurred grumblings and gripings as people knew Enosila's rambling, conflated ways and were suspicious of where this might lead.

"Order, please order in the assembly," demanded Hannah.

"Order."

"The floor recognizes the Honorable Member of the Upper Area, Enosila."

Enosila rose to his feet and slowly strutted back and forth before those seated at the Executive Table. Huffing and puffing, he began slowly, using his exasperating monotone approach and exaggerating by pausing after each sentence.

"Governor, the proposed plan is commendable, quite commendable indeed, and has potential, albeit slim, potential for the preconceived positive outcomes. This deception may fool the populace of Ecaps, or at least the majority of Pati'na's family, and perhaps, yes, perhaps, even some gullible friends."

Now, he was banging his hand on the speaker dais.

"However, this hallow expectation at first blush, can not be, but yet it is, for this horse to accept an amateurish impostor, vastly unprepared and totally ignoring the emotional connection between horse and rider."

Then, even further, sarcastically continued looking skyward for some divine intervention.

"Do you have any unknown form of identification for this horse with no legs, a simple identifiable badge perhaps?"

"A horse's ass, I say to your weak assumption."

"I, Enosila, believe this presumption of deception is doomed to fail, doomed even before it begins."

Spinning around facing the villagers, now blazingly bellowing, "Because when this mount, this Eaus'eche, when this filly is tested, she will never be scammed by your under-rated exploit in this manner."

Enosila paused momentarily, seemingly relishing in his moment in the light, then continued, performing a rendition that even the Greater Sage Grouse would be proud of.

"You may be successful in tricking this horse's seemingly adequate vision, perhaps tricking her sense of smell, but, yes, I say again, the emotional bond between Pati'na and Eaus'eche seems insurmountable from my astute unbiased perspective!"

An enormous uproar filled the assembly, with many calling for Enosila's expulsion from the crowd as he took his seat.

"Point of order."

"Point of personal privilege."

Others demand that Enosila 'be shot on the spot'.

Coupled with the pent-up stress, these comments finally exploded into a flurry of malaise, threats, and demands, consuming any semblance of control and straying further from the assembly's primary objective.

Finally, in desperation, Vexiana requested a point of personal privilege while trying to redirect the assembled.

"Order, order, now, do not test me, or I will clear the gallery," affirmed Hannah. The floor recognizes My Lady Vexiana for comment.

Vexiana started calmly, trying to return civility to the meeting, stating, "I don't condone Enosila's arrogant performance, not in the least, but I agree with his reasoning. Therefore, I propose we conceive a plan to gather and access some of Pati'na's worn clothing, preserving her scent. With me dressed in these articles of Pati'na's clothing, this could very well be the method of deceiving even an astute filly like Eaus'eche."

Hannah again took the gavel and attempted to establish order.

"Thank you, Enosila, for your comments. We will take them under advisement as we continue to discuss resolving the emotional aspect between a horse and its rider."

With that, the scheduling of further meetings brought the adjournment of the meeting.

The committee agreed to make a plan in an attempt to have someone they know be hired by Ecaps as the stable groom housing Eaus'eche while observing Pati'na's habits and daily routine.

Hannah clarified that there would undoubtedly be the only opportunity to access the dry-water.

After adjourning the meeting in the assembly hall, she asked that the governor, Elders, and military and security leaders remain to continue discussions and construct a plan of action.

The leaders of the military and security stressed that information on the stable's layout, Pati'na's actions and routine, and the security surveillance of all these factors would be essential for any possible means of success.

The governor noted that he knew that a stable hands position was available in Ecaps and that the need for a stable groom had been posted. The Elders agree that this would be an ideal outcome if it were possible to find a candidate from Unknowns who won't draw any suspicion with his or her application.

Hannah decided to close the meeting as fatigue was evident, and any further discussion would be futile and damaging to those participating well beyond expectations.

# The Kidnapping

After consideration of the various candidates, the committee opted to have Rabin become the one to apply for the stable groom position in Ecaps, as he regularly crossed over these territorial boundaries while playing with other children from Ecaps.

Another reason for his selection was young Rabin's instinct to act like a fool while entertaining and amusing his family and friends. He gave the impression of being slow-witted, but the exact opposite was the reality of his bright, clever mind.

If chosen to work in the stables as the groom, a boy with an assumed simple mind and inept behavior would also have a better chance of going unnoticed, becoming nearly invisible, and of minor to no concern to others.

Fortunately, he did become the stable groom. Rabin blended in as expected, and soon Pati'na had taken a shine to this young, enthusiastic, quiet boy. Pati'na's daily routine varied minimally on most days, except when she would take Eaus'eche with her when she resupplied the dry-water.

"I really like being the stable groom at the Ecaps stables, Pati'na. You take good care of your horse; she is very lucky to have you as her friend."

"It's been good to have you working here at the stables too, Rabin. Eaus'eche seems to be getting accustomed to being around, and I like how you keep everything clean and neat."

As time passed, people started recognizing Rabin as a regular presence in and around the stable area. This helped him move freely beyond the immediate stables and explore all the possible paths Vexiana could choose on the day of the kidnapping.

Another you boy, Byron, who delivered the hay to the stables, also became friends with Rabin. With Byron from Ecaps, he knew many lesser-known trails and shortcuts around the stables.

One day, Rabin helped Byron stow the hay in the barn. Rabin mentioned how neat this old barn was, and Byron boasted,

"I'll show you something that is the neatest of all, Rabin, and I bet you can't tell me that you know something neater."

Byron moved an old wooden ladder at the back of the barn, exposing a small door.

"Rabin, this is the emergency escape tunnel entrance inside the hay barn that eventually exits into the surrounding forest."

"Wow, that is the neatest, alright, Byron, really neat. I don't know anything neater than this, that's for sure, thanks."

When the opportunity came, Rabin would return to the hay barn and follow the tunnel to where it ended and how near its location was to the Unknowns area.

Pati'na showed Rabin how Eaus'eche liked to be handled and what she found irritating and usually balked at. Rabin noted all of these traits and eventually discovered that the location of the exit from the tunnel was easily accessed from the Unknowns compound.

Pati'na's most obvious habit was the apple and carrot treat she offered Eaus'eche every time she visited the stables. Rabin used this same wooden bucket to gather apples and carrots, making it a definite asset during the final deception and kidnapping of Eaus'eche. He also managed to assemble small articles of clothing that Pati'na would discard absentmindedly around the stable area.

The amount of information Rabin had gathered far exceeded Hannah's expectations, and now they knew the location of the entrance to the tunnel, which brought them right inside Ecap's hay barn. This meant that Vexiana could quickly enter Ecaps without being detected right into the stables.

Despite this newfound good fortune, Hannah decided to continue with her deception plan by having some of the Military Guards create a distraction, enough to rouse the Ecaps Sentries and draw attention to the far side of Ecaps, away from the location housing the stables. Although Vexiana could use the tunnel to enter the stable area, she could not take Eaus'eche back through the tunnel and would be exposed for a period of time.

Rabin led Vexiana to the tunnel entrance and reviewed the layout of the stables one more time. It was just as Rabin had described as Vexiana found herself inside the hay barn within the stable area. She anxiously waited to hear the disturbance indicating it would be time to kidnap Pati'na's stupid horse with no legs, a horse she never liked.

Waiting was forever as she saw two sentries posted within the stable area.

Meanwhile, the Unknowns' Guards had not been able to attract enough action from the Ecaps Sentries, provoking them to investigate this minor disturbance. The sergeant knew that anything too big would trigger a full alert, shutting down all the entrances to Ecaps and, more importantly, adding more security to their stables and jeopardizing the kidnapping plan.

The suggestion was to leave behind a small group of volunteers and have them try to provoke some of the sentries by faking an attack from the Klongs, hoping they would assume that these people in danger were people from Ecaps. With the Klongs getting more aggressive recently, it might work.

Three volunteers remained in the area with the remainder of the party held up in case the plan went south, and the volunteers needed rescuing.

Vexiana heard the disturbance and watched as the two sentries left their post and went outside the stable area. Cautiously, Vexiana left the barn and entered the stables, looking for Eaus'eche's stall.

Vexiana found everything as Rabin had described: the bucket used for the apples and carrots and the horse equipment, including the bridle, bit, reins, and two water pouches.

Vexiana silently led Eaus'eche slowly, steadily out from the stable area by her bridle, and bit with the wooden fruit bucket securely in hand.

After the guards received the signal that Vexiana had successfully executed the kidnapping mission, the commander responsible for creating the diversion retreated with his elite troops, returning to the compound as planned.

Vexiana carefully led Eaus'eche into her new stable, still astonished that the plan went undetected without a single hitch as the Elite Armed Security Forces quickly secured the Unknowns' stable area, particularly Eaus'eche's surroundings.

At daybreak, Pati'na awoke as usual to start her day. Still, her womanly instincts distantly sensed red flags, indicating something was off or wrong.

Yerlaw, who is usually punctual and predictable, hadn't updated her on the current dry-water supply status, which was odd; why hadn't he done so? This oversight was one of many nagging red flags.

Upon entering the stables, Pati'na was alarmed to discover that Eaus'eche's stall door was left open and noticed several items were missing in the paddock area.

Now cautious, she continued toward Eaus'eche's stall, shocked and dumbfounded when she became aware that it was empty.

In an instant state of panic, turning about, she found herself face-to-face with her reflection.

Staring in bewilderment, Pati'na initially was at a loss for words.

"You, Vexiana?"

"Are you responsible for this?"

"You are more than an evil wicket woman, Vexiana."

Pati'na, now furiously striking out at Vexiana in her state of panic,

"You'll pay for this with your very existence."

Exhibiting a controlling posture, Vexiana holds up her hand, "Before acting too irrationally, Pati'na, please hear me out."

"We have no intention of harming your beloved horse, Eaus'eche."

Vexiana carefully watched for Pati'na's reaction before continuing.

"Hannah only has one request."

"Take her to the location of the dry-water, then Eaus'eche will be harmlessly returned to you."

Pati'na, now starting to focus on what was happening, exhibited more self-control, "A simple request, Vexiana. You must have been playing among those Slugmucks again."

Vexiana, acting like a scolding teacher, pointed directly at Pati'na, exclaiming!

"You have three days to decide, Pati'na, three days. Remember, Pati'na, you hold Eaus'eche's fate in your hands. Yes, you alone, Pati'na, will dictate how this situation ends."

Pati'na tried to contain her trembling, acknowledging the situation while trying to remain lucid. "You don't have the right to do this, Vexiana. This is heartless, and you are more like my damn sister than my cousin; how could you do this? You know I can't now or ever agree to this, Vexiana. You already know that."

Starting to walk away, Vexiana smugly turned.

"Fine, now you only have two days, Pati'na. Do you want to try for one day? This is not a game, Pati'na. Think wisely. And Pati'na, do not mention this to anyone, especially your Kenja."

Pati'na remained standing in utter shock and disbelief. Vexiana fled into the wooded area behind the stables.

Pati'na dreadfully realized that this situation was more catastrophic than Vexiana or the Unknowns could imagine.

The Unknowns kidnapped Eaus'eche because they believed that Pati'na knew the secret of locating the dry-water and would reveal it if they held Eaus'eche hostage. Pati'na knew that the Unknowns wouldn't harm Eaus'eche and that Eaus'eche had been trained not to disclose any information; the grave was the final destination for this information.

While entering the stable looking for Pati'na, Kenja noticed someone sprinting away from Pati'na, heading toward the wooded area that lined the stables.

Looking back toward Pati'na, Kenja noticed how motionless she stood. She looked confused and fearful while remaining totally unaware of Kenja.

Kenja called out, startling Pati'na. "Oh, what's wrong, Pati'na?"

Pati'na was sorely exhibiting an anxiety profoundly etched on her face.

"Who was that running away from you, Pati'na?"

Pati'na burst into tears and broke down emotionally, hugging Kenja as she trembled and uncontrollably shaking and openly distraught.

"What is it, Pati'na? What's going on here?"

Pati'na was now struggling emotionally while holding onto a hitching post, trying not to hyperventilate, "I can't tell you, Kenja. I can't tell anyone."

Taking Pati'na firmly by her shoulders, "Pati'na, whenever I hear these words, it, without fail, always indicates the exact opposite with a dire need to confide in someone you can trust."

Pati'na was shaking her head, no.

"I can't, Kenja, I just can't. Not just yet, anyhow."

Trying to compose herself.

"I'll consult with my Fate-Keepers, but only if I feel there is no other option."

"Pati'na, even these words suggest that this issue involves more than just you."

Pati'na continues to struggle free, ridding herself of Kenja's grasp;

"Pati'na, listen, stop it for one second, and just listen. So often, you have asked me to put my trust in you at various times on my journey here in Modeerf, and I have. Now, you must take a leap of faith and put your trust in me."

# The Disruption

Upon returning to Ecaps, Kenja was consumed with concern for Pati'na. What could have caused her to be so devastated and overwhelmed?

Even before arriving in Ecaps, Kenja noticed the anxiety on people's faces and some running ahead to reveal Pati'na's confused and disoriented state.

A somber mood blanketed us as we entered the Fate-Keepers Lodge, where the council had terminated their meeting, vacating the hall to meet with Pati'na's parents, Sawenco and Yada.

The Fate-Keepers promptly summoned Yerlaw the Defender, Jonfrei the Pathfinder, and the Elder's Council of Ecaps to an emergency meeting.

Ignoring protocol, Ecaps Chief of Council Enosewi got straight to the point and called the meeting to prevent the squandering of crucial time or opportunities.

Meanwhile, the citizens of Ecaps continued gathering outside the Assembly Hall, curious and concerned about the immediate assembly of so many prominent leaders.

As more awareness of the seriousness and extent of the matter unfolded, more and more citizens sat in disbelief as the tale of Eaus'eche's kidnapping emerged, to their horror.

Sheer panic and disturbing chaos soon erupted as deep shock and despair caused many to brutally interrupt and shout insults at each other in an alarming, agitated, and ugly manner.

Unopposed, anxiety and doom quickly ruled the day. The tension and elevated despair brought the whole thing to the level of a massive powder keg, where one small flint was all it would take for total anarchy and lawlessness to erupt, something that has been absent in Ecaps since its inception at the beginning of dawn, the genesis of Modeerf.

With the Chief of Council, Enosewi again repeatedly called for 'Order'.

The pounding of the gavel was barely audible amidst the abnormal, disturbing, and inflammatory nature of these citizens of Ecaps.

"Order."

The gavel is now pounding out a terrifying beat, usually associated with an Apache War Cry. This sound would make anyone's blood run cold if only they could hear it.

"We must have order."

After seemingly countless efforts to regain even a reasonable semblance of control, Enosewi finally, pleading in desperation, appeared to bring partial order and civility back to the assembly.

In their apparent despair, people continued a muted grumblingly, seated in a now uncommunicative state of bleak and dismal emptiness filled with a grave and fearful concern.

Enosewi cautiously continued while watching concerning pockets of tension throughout the hall for possible disturbances erupting again.

"All is not lost unless you continue to panic and we, your leaders, are not panicking. No, we have never faced a setback like this. I never even imagined something like this. But now would be the worst time for us not to listen or abide by the Fate-Keepers."

Taking a deep breath, hoping for sensibility to become recognized, Enosewi continued, "At this point, let me be obvious. The Unknowns are still unaware that by kidnapping Eaus'eche, they have unwittingly achieved their goal of securing a means of locating the dry-water."

"Having Eaus'eche securely housed in their stables, this fact is troubling as we enter unchartered waters. However, we also know that no harm will come to her as this situation continues."

Zaluum, the eldest and notably the most respected Elder, considered by many the wisest, most learned man of Modeerf, humbly rose from his chair and asked for permission to address the assembly.

With Zaluum rising to his feet, this act alone altered the temperature and climate of those gathered in the auditorium.

Enosewi stood, confirming Zaluum's request.

"The Floor Recognizes the Honorable House Elder, Zaluum of Knightsburg."

Zaluum painfully grimaced and stood, picking up his notes and holding them before him. Then he began.

"I have not yet formulated a plan establishing the safe return of Eaus'eche, and I do concede, as is often recorded in history, that this could well be the last battle between good and evil before our Day of Judgment, this traumatic issue encompasses our very existence here on Modeerf."

*Observing Zaluum's troubled face, he seemed to be staring squarely into an infinite abyss with the semblance of someone about to witness eternity's destruction.*

"However, I don't need any time to ponder the grave impact of these Unknown's actions, which will undoubtedly reveal unimaginable consequences."

"What concerns me even more than them locating the dry-water and accessing it is the probability that, if they ever achieved their intent, they will surely lack the necessary skills, experience, nor knowledge in its safe extraction or transport."

"Removing the dry-water from this facility will have catastrophic if not even greater consequential results for Modeerf and quite possibly the established universe, causing a redistribution of orbits in the universes balance, one that all eternity itself might be incapable of rectifying."

Noting the facial expressions of his audience, demonstrating that his intent is registering, Zaluum becomes seated.

A continuing aura of hopelessness blanketed the ancient chamber; with the razor-sharp wit and harsh truth just spoken, the attendees fell silent in this scene of gloominess, in this circle of despair.

Zaluum's warning made it clear that failure to take immediate corrective action would result in severe and irreversible consequences. This failure alone could trigger a chain reaction of events that may only be diverted by an improbable divine intervention if one exists.

At one point, I thought about approaching Pati'na to attempt to console her, but fortunately, my little inner voice intervened. This thought would have undoubtedly been the worst action for me to take at this point.

With the assembly officially adjourning, the Fate-Keepers remained to discuss open strategies that needed review. Considering the opinions submitted, the consensus concluded that Pati'na should arrange a rogue meeting with Vexiana and Hannah to discuss the release of Eaus'eche in exchange for information about the potential whereabouts of the dry-water.

# Discovering the Secret

Hannah realized that it would take significant time for the Ecaps leaders to devise a feasible plan for their recapture of Eaus'eche. After strengthening the already impressive fortification with even more sentries posted to thwart the anticipated retaliation, Hannah directed everyone to stand down except for the active sentries, using this time to provide some much-needed rest.

A weary Vexiana headed to her lodge, heading to bed and some much-needed rest. Despite feeling so totally spent, somehow she knew it would be one of those nights where sleep would become painfully evasive.

Thinking back to her recent encounter with Pati'na and Kenja, she remembers how strikingly handsome this Kenja from Earth was and how lucky her cousin Pati'na was to have connected with him.

As she suspected, sleep was hopelessly elusive, so she researched some old documents about Earth. She remembered that her great-grandfather had once mentioned that, unlike Modeerf, Earth has many languages.

Reflecting on her childhood and this particular story that her great-grandfather Lenden had told her. This story was also about a visitor from Earth who spoke French. He fell ill and was taken care of by the Mother's Maids. After he recovered, he started farming and created beautiful, fertile gardens where he grew truly amazing 'out-of-the-ordinary' vegetables, sharing his knowledge with anyone interested.

He named the area Terrebonne, which loosely translates from French to 'good earth', and the lake 'Grande Eau' or 'Big Water', which later became known by the locals as Lake Gran'oh.

Vexiana continued trying to get her eyes to become heavy and bring on some much-needed sleep. She continued reading more interesting facts her great-grandfather had logged in his journals. She was intrigued by this past French connection.

During Vexiana's research for insight into any French connections to Modeerf, she came across a word oddly familiar to her but one that initially she couldn't make any connection to. The term was 'eau', which, when translated into English, means 'water'. Anything relating to water was always of interest to Vexiana and worthy of further investigation.

Vexiana was trying to find a connection between the words 'Grande Eau' and 'Eaus'eche'. She eventually realized that the first three letters of 'Eaus'eche' were 'eau', which meant 'water' in French. This stirred her curiosity to look into the rest of the letters, 's'eche', which she soon discovered meant 'dry' in English.

She looked down at the paper where she wrote out the translation for' Eaus'eche', realizing the indirect translation meant; 'dry-water'.

Vexiana was floored by what lay before her, not knowing whether to laugh or cry.

It was Eaus'eche, the weird, stupid horse with no legs, all this time. This revelation went from simply being an insane possibility to an all-time sleight of hand, an illusion of sorts that revealed Eaus'eche, who knew how to access the location and detect the dry-water.

Like a ton of bricks, it registered that the Unknowns already had the key to dry-water. The fact that Eaus'eche held the answer to the dry-water riddle meant Pati'na herself was no longer a player in the game. They had already captured the Queen.

Now fully awake and fully electrified with her new insight, Vexiana had the sentries go to find Hannah.

When told about Vexiana's discovery, Hannah was absolutely stunned and speechless for the first time in a very long time.

"I think you'll have to explain all of this to me again; I just want to be sure it's all not just a dream."

Her face slowly went from total bewilderment and confusion to deep suspicion and amazement. I was amazed at how long this horse with no legs deception had passed undetected.

She was still shaking her head in disbelief, but her mind. Her mind was now working on a conscious plan to accomplish her lifelong ambition, a mission resulting in the Unknowns assuming complete and total control of the dry-water. And Modeerf itself.

# The New Dilemma

The Elders and Group Leaders convened an emergency meeting in the Unknowns Assembly Hall. Despite everyone's near-total exhaustion, the community responded to the urgent call. The rumored talk among the citizens was about a substantial and positive change to improve their health and suspected future, as evidenced by their steadily increasing fragility.

After Vexiana's presentation, Hannah explained how Vexiana's research had exposed a new situation and its potential outcomes. Then revealed that this knowledge had also unearthed a new and perplexing reality, creating a new dilemma that must be addressed immediately for any means of a possible positive outcome.

"We now know conclusively that Pati'na's horse Eaus'eche holds the key to dry-water, not Pati'na as we previously assumed."

Wanting to establish the significance of what she was about to say, Hannah first turned to acknowledge the Elders and Group Leaders in attendance, then returning to face the assembled, Hannah began;

"This fact alone has made for a complete and necessary alteration in our plans."

With her fingers slowly drumming on the desktop, contemplating, she chose her words carefully to ensure clarity.

"We must continue to convince the people and, more so, the leaders of Ecaps that we still believe Pati'na holds the key to the dry-water and that she alone is still the main objective for our kidnapping of Eaus'eche."

Hannah patiently waited for the murmurs to die down before speaking. She emphasized that the opportunity was a now-only possibility leading to a definite reality. Not only was their survival at stake, but it was also a once-in-a-lifetime chance to gain complete control of the dry-water and ultimately rule over Modeerf.

"Listen. Please, listen up, people, and hear me out."

Hannah again waited patiently for the room to quiet down and for people to refocus.

"Without exception, we must all, every one of us, continue doing exactly as we would before this awareness."

"Look to the person to your left and then to the person on your right and say to each of them;"

"I need you. Can I count on you?"

"All of us must become of one mind, with one objective."

Hannah's ability to read and motivate an audience was fully engaged at this very moment, captivating and motivating.

"This new plan has an even greater expectation of success than our original proposal in our long-term stability and ensuring a long-term healthy existence"

"So, don't despair; our day of reckoning is at hand, as the future, our future has never looked brighter for each and every one of us."

Hannah's speech was met with a boisterous and exuberant acceptance, "For all of us Unknowns," echoed through the Assembly Hall.

"For all of us, for all Unknowns."

Among the abundance of voiced jubilation with those in attendance, one voice of discontentment remained, demanding to speak.

Enosila stood and began his well-known pretentious posturing:

"Madam, point of personal privilege."

"Madam, please, point of personal privilege."

"Please, Madam."

Hannah stood looking exasperated but ceded to her obligation.

"The floor recognizes Enosila's point of personal privilege."

Enosila once again started strutting about, prancing like a peacock fanning out its spectacular tail feathers, its colorful train, and began with the custom of 'train rattling' in front of the Councilors' table like the pompous ass he was perceived to be.

Enosila turned around unexpectedly, almost losing his balance to the delight of many, and quickly regained his composure. Still, this was probably more of a deliberate stunt to create a dramatic visual effect than a misstep.

"What in the blazes reason could you possibly have for thinking that Eaus'eche will willingly lead you to this secret location?"

He slams his hand down on the table, obviously once again for more effect, while now looking up at the heavens as if the answer would magically appear for all to see.

"This would seem unfathomable for me to accept without a plan."

Desperately searching his pockets for a plan, "One which appears to be under wraps at the moment. If, that's if, indeed, there is a plan."

Hannah, now becoming thoroughly irritated, stands, interrupting Enosila.

"We have a complete and detailed plan of action, Enosila, which has more than merely a perceived positive outcome. If you will please be seated, thank you."

Hannah waited for Enosila to grudgingly be seated before continuing, "At your 'much-disguised' insistence questioning the very existence of our plan and its success probability, upon which I will now elaborate."

"The plan begins with Vexiana disguising herself as Pati'na and entering the stable where Eaus'eche is located. Then, during the course of grooming her, along with all of the other small talk that Pati'na usually uses, she will mention that the dry-water supply in Ecaps is running low and the probability of a trip to replenish the dry-water is in the making."

Hannah showed her growing displeasure with Enosila with her finger menacingly pointing directly at him.

"This, Enosila, is only assuming this so-called potential bond exists between horse and rider and is one that might be wise not to ignore regardless of my position on the matter. Can I trust that this satisfies your concern?"

Enosila rose again, to the displeasure of many, and caused a disgruntled disruption, asking for one more point of personal privilege.

Gruffly repeating the request.

"Madam, Madam, a point of personal privilege."

Enosila, not now waiting for confirmation to continue, began, "You dare to stand here before us and expect us to believe that you intend to deceive this horse for a second time with the same scenario, which indicates to me that it is also your opinion that we are even more gullible than that old-nag presently housed in one for our stable stalls, to which, I think you believe us to be the horse's ass in this case."

A significant outbreak of discontent toward Enosila erupted again.

Hannah called for order.

Then continued, "Sometimes, Enosila, you cause me to accept this likelihood," motioning to Enosila to be seated; "Our success hinges on Dr. Zeplyn's expertise. She is our lead scientist at the Mediator facility and is currently finalizing the formulation of a drug that will be given to Eaus'eche before Vexiana reaches the stable."

Hannah paused before continuing. The villagers also started vocally muttering about Enosila and his often unwanted and unwarranted interruptions.

"He's such a long-winded big bag of hot air sometimes."

"Yes, ever since he came across that damn dictionary, he feels obligated to."

"Give us a break, Enosila, just sit down and shut up, listen for once, okay?"

"Maybe try sitting down if listening is too much for you."

"That's if you can find a means to control your unwanted tantrums."

Hannah stepped in, "Order, we will show respect to everyone gathered here with the realization that all this is coming at everyone so quickly. But above all, we must remain civil to one another."

Letting her words be absorbed, she then continued, "My special forces team and I will trail behind Vexiana, ready to step in if needed. Once we have completed our mission of securing the dry-water, we'll relay our success back to our compound leaders confirming this fact. We will unite by re-assembling at Tignish Pond, re-establishing the glory of our native land while asserting full control of Modeerf."

Feeling confident her message has been well received, Hannah continued, "Undoubtedly, during this period, the Ecaps Guards and their neighboring military allies will be attacking our compound, only to realize that they have been deceived. They will soon understand that they have a new master to serve and must now obey the Ruling Unknowns."

Hannah tried to continue, competing with the many triumphant outbursts. "When they arrive at our compound, and they will most certainly arrive, I want our Leading Commander to greet them with a white flag, telling them that we now possess both access and control of the dry-water."

Hannah was now standing boldly, with her new assured confidence added.

"There is no need for any more bloodshed unless they decide to exercise their option to do so, as it is their option. May they make the wiser decision of the two."

With that, Hannah adjourned the assembly.

Vexiana, Hannah, and two other high-ranking officials visited Dr. Zeplyn at the Mediator facility for an update on her attempt to create the proper drug needed to pacify Eaus'eche to a state of becoming submissive.

Meanwhile, Vexiana walked to her lodge to change into the same clothing she wore when she kidnapped Eaus'eche. Later, she returned to the center, where she met with Hannah and Dr. Zeplyn.

Vexiana questioned her appearance, "Well, what do you think?"

Hannah's big grin had now returned as Vexiana pirouetted in Pati'na's outfit.

"Well, yes. Yes indeed. Pati'na, you are properly dressed for your rendezvous with Eaus'eche to retrieve the elusive dry-water."

After administering the first dosage, Dr. Zeplyn observed that it had the intended effects on Eaus'eche and caused no apparent side effects. Meanwhile, Pati'na waited patiently in an area adjacent to the stables.

Once fully awake, yet still groggy, Vexiana took Eaus'eche's reins and led her out of the stall, informing Hannah that they needed a couple of water pouches to transport the dry-water. Vexiana had noticed two water pouches on the wall in the Ecaps stables, but unfortunately, leaving them behind was an oversight.

Hannah assured her not to worry.

"I have some water pouches. I'll return to the stable, get two, and catch up to you, Pati'na."

In the vicinity of Eaus'eche, Hannah kept consciously referring to Vexiana as Pati'na.

"Keep slowly heading along the trail, Pati'na, since it seems you have already gained Eaus'eche's trust and confidence."

As they walked along the trail, Hannah and the Sentries followed Vexiana at a safe distance until they reached Daydream Waterfalls.

There, Vexiana paused, allowing Eaus'eche to rest and drink, until she noticed Hannah getting irritated and impatient. Hannah kept urging her to move on because of the urgency of the matter.

As Vexiana approached the Tangled Garden, memories of a naive time in her life and better memories of her upbringing flooded in, reminding her of her youth when she used to go with Pati'na and their friends to gather crops for their parents.

A deep sadness filled Vexiana's heart as she reflected on the misplaced choices she had made in her life since those days and how they had led her down an irresponsible path that brought her to this precise moment.

Eaus'eche suddenly stopped bringing Vexiana back to the present moment. The horse with no legs appeared anxious while prancing at the edge of a small pool of water, quickly exhibiting traits before leaping, wanting to jump in.

Uncertain of what to expect, Vexiana watched as Eaus'eche approached the edge of the pool and leaped into the water.

Clutching onto the reins, Vexiana followed, encountering roaring energy currents and struggling to maintain contact with Eaus'eche and, eventually, surfacing inside a colossal cave with Eaus'eche still in hand.

At first, she became aware of an irritating buzzing as though all of the bees in Modeerf were inside this cave, then abruptly, to a total deathly corpse-like silence. Awestruck and unsure, she waited for Hannah and the Sentries to resurface.

They, too, emerged from the surface inside the cave, also seemingly overwhelmed by the magnificent sight before them.

It was evident that Hannah and the senior officers were still determining their next move on how or even where to navigate this enormous cave with its cluster of cells and chambers.

Once more, they acknowledged that without any other option, they were destined to rely on Eaus'eche to guide them from each section and only hope that she located the dry-water sooner rather than later.

One of the sentries stopped and seemed fixated on listening to something.

Noticing this, Hannah questioned the young Sentry.

"What do you hear?"

"That's just it, Madam."

Still straining to hear.

"It's what I don't hear, Madam."

Hannah's puzzled look questioned him again.

"Madam, I don't hear any echoes, Madam."

After acknowledging this, Hannah motioned them to continue following Eaus'eche in pursuit of their objective. She often had previously heard talk of an Echoless Cave but always dismissed it as folklore.

Not lost was the enormity of this Echoless Cave as Hannah's sense of success waned a little more with each chamber unsuccessfully searched, knowing that their objective would soon become known and the counteraction to follow.

Vexiana suddenly squealed and excitedly pointed to Eaus'eche, now hesitating by a small pool, exhibiting emotions one usually connects with success; Vexiana went to her knees and touched the water.

She raised her head, witnessing everyone desperately waiting.

"Is it dry-water, Vexiana?"

Vexiana raised her hands in jubilation;

"The Great Spirit is with us, Hannah. Our prayers have been answered, Yahoo!"

At the top of her lungs, she was shouting as she once did in her youth.

"We've done it, we've done it, Hannah! This is it, and there is no doubt about this being anything other than the elusive dry-water."

After a brief but well-earned celebration, Hannah expressed again that they must complete their mission as quickly as possible.

Knowing now, without a doubt, all control of Modeerf was at hand, and all eternity awaited confirmation of their success back at Tignish Pond to commemorate and celebrate this historic feat.

They cautiously filled the two water pouches with the precious dry-water, attempting to control their excitement.

The Unknowns had not had dry-water in their possession for eons, let alone the possibility of having dominating power with this newly acquired commodity and complete control over dry-water.

Hannah raised her hand in commemoration, "Today, our sovereignty over the control of dry-water will be landmarked as a historic day for the modern Unknowns of Modeerf."

# Nearing the End

Meanwhile, back at the Unknowns Headquarters, as Hannah and Vexiana filled the two water pouches with dry-water, the United Forces of Ecaps and the militaries of the surrounding communities stormed the Unknowns compound with the intent of rescuing Eaus'eche from her kidnappers.

This advancement party, being unopposed, quickly made its way through the main entrance of the Unknowns compound, unexpectedly meeting with little to no resistance, only to be greeted by the Unknowns' Leading Commander, holding a white flag in the air and waving it vigorously to ensure its visibility.

As planned, the Ecaps United Forces encircled and contained the Unknowns' compound; this unexpected sight of the white flag caused some valid initial confusion among their commanders about its intent or, more likely, possible deception.

After discussing this unexpected tactic, the Ecaps leadership temporarily accepted the white flag and communicated before proceeding with the planned assault on the Unknowns' compound.

While ordering his troops to stand down, the Unknowns' Leading Commander asked to speak directly with Pati'na and the Fate-Keepers about the current situation.

Informing the commander of the United Forces of Ecaps that the Unknowns now possessed the means to access the location of the dry-water and that Hannah and Vexiana were presently on their way there, making no need for further violence or bloodshed to protect something already compromised.

Pati'na was horrified as she realized that the two 'dry-water' pouches were still in the stall where they belonged; in the morning, she discovered Eaus'eche was missing. It was one thing to notice that her bridle, bit, and reins were also gone, but these two pouches were the only safe way to transport the dry-water.

The fact that these two vital water pouches were still hanging on their dowels by the stall entrance and were the only two water pouches designed and capable of safely transporting the dry-water was terrifying, causing immediate panic for Pati'na.

Looking at Pati'na, Kenja had never seen such a look of absolute and utter terror on anyone's face, the terror usually associated with an Armageddon movie.

"What is it, Pati'na?"

Kenja cautiously shook Pati'na's shoulders, returning her to the present moment. She was still in a very confused state of near spellbinding hysteria, with her entire being severely shaking, exhibiting signs of stress overload.

"What's wrong, Pati'na?"

Pati'na was now uncontrollably trembling like a massive, rapidly building volcano whose eruption seemed imminent. Kenja sensed that she could shortly be going into convulsions.

"It's the dry-water, Kenja, it's the dry-water."

"Okay, Pati'na, take a deep breath and calmly tell me more. What about the dry-water?"

Appearing to be bombarded with constant unwanted visions, Pati'na continued stammering.

"They're making a big mistake, Kenja. Severe destruction is inevitable, which will be horrific, Kenja, just horrific."

Pati'na seemed grievously close to hyperventilating.

"I told you before, Kenja, that the dry-water is only stable within the cave and has to be safely transported in the designated two dry-water pouches."

Starting to stutter and tending to stammer, Pati'na was visibly close to a complete meltdown.

"The two water pouches I said to you were vital; they still hang back in the Ecaps stables, Kenja."

Kenja noticed the initial shock partially ebbing as Pati'na seemingly focused her thought process, and her breathing became less erratic.

"Once removed from the Echoless Cave and not stored in the proper pouches, this unstable energy is guaranteed to intensify, building to a deadly catastrophic explosion."

Pati'na pleaded with their Leading Commander to find a way to intervene, "Is there any possible way to reach Hannah and Vexiana, any means at all?"

Grasping the seriousness of this ominous situation, the Leading Commander confirms that there are no means of contacting Hannah or Vexiana as shear pandemonium and chaos spread throughout the troops within earshot.

"Let's fly, Kenja. United, the two of us can soar together. We may be the only remaining chance to prevent the destruction of Modeerf and, ultimately, the inevitable disruption of the universe."

Despite the futility of the mission, Kenja persisted in helping Pati'na prepare for the battle against Vexiana and Hannah to recover Eaus'eche despite the anxiety and stress that caused him to sense an acute explosive pain in his chest.

As they flew high overhead, they quickly spotted Vexiana frighteningly walking Eaus'eche outside the Echoless Cave, still carrying the two suspect pouches strapped to her back containing a ticking time bomb harboring catastrophic consequences.

Spotting Pati'na and Kenja unexpectedly descending upon them, the sentries became terrified, opting for disastrous and unwanted results with panic among the ranks.

Complete chaos ensued, and the sentries gravely underestimating the strength of a horse with no legs proved disastrous.

Eaus'eche bolted, attempting to rid herself of her captives.

One of the terrified sentries thrust his lance, piercing Eaus'eche's neck, seriously wounding her.

This action was all the stimulus needed to trigger an eruption, provoking an onslaught of cuts and slashes from the sentries, mercilessly killing Eaus'eche.

Pati'na's perceived attempt at any rescue evaporated, now witnessing Eaus'eche's lifeless body tragically falling into an abyss, still with the two pouches firmly strapped to her back.

Even with the foreseeable and inevitable explosion, Pati'na fought Vexiana and Hannah, fueled by personal furious rage and vengeance.

Dreadfully, during the continuing chaos, Kenja received another large gash in his sternum.

With an axe impaling his chest, all physical resistance ended as it immediately rendered Kenja inept.

"Run and jump, Kenja, run and jump off the face of this abyss. Believe in the presence of your grandfather, and fly."

"Pati'na, I'm too exhausted; I'm spent and can't fly, not with this huge crack in my sternum."

"You can fly, Kenja, heal yourself and fly if you believe in yourself. You can do this; you alone will determine whether you survive or die."

*Kenja recognized the energy hurdling toward him. It was Grandfather WiKenja, nearing like a bolt of lightning.*

WiKenja's voice weak from exhaustion, now frail, with little strength left cried out with anxiety, "I've been searching for you, Kenja. For an eternity."

Pati'na's final words were reverberating with intentions and direction, "Watch for Celeste; she will guide you to the porthole and a safe place, Kenja. I feel you, Kenja. I will feel your madness for all eternity. Go now! Go and jump now and find your truth!"

It was heartbreaking to witness the destruction of Modeerf and the tragic, horrifying loss of Pati'na's beloved Eaus'eche.

However, the most agonizing part was seeing Pati'na herself reduced to dust. Her last act before her demise was thrusting me through the one remaining porthole out of Modeerf.

The energy of Kenja's grandfather continued journeying with Kenja on his quest home and kept repeating, "Stay focused, Kenja! Concentrate on the bright white lights ahead of you. Spotting the brightest light is your beacon and will guide you like your red-tailed hawk leading you safely home."

Kenja's encouragement grew, clearly sensing the needed wisdom of his Grandmother Dawnlilly, "Don't think, Kenja, Paint."

Kenja was utterly unprepared for the intense and terrifying turbulence he faced next.

It was like being caught in an unforgiving current, mimicking a menacing crushing rip-tide, one continually demanding extensive energy that Kenja didn't have.

Kenja clearly became delirious, being bombarded by hallucinations from all directions, sensing that someone or something was in the process of harvesting his heart like it was being ripped from his chest and discarded.

Pati'na's voice echoed in his mind. "Keep Celeste's image before you, Kenja. You are my truth, Kenja. You will forever be my truth, Kenja."

# Kenja's Close Encounter

Anthony briefly regained consciousness, lying on what seemed to be a hospital stretcher. He was still disoriented and unable to process what was happening around him. He was unaware of his whereabouts, and his exhaustion was overwhelming, forcing him to succumb to sleep once more. He was no longer in control and was at the mercy of the shadows surrounding him.

Anthony attempted to open his eyes, but he couldn't focus on anything. Instead, he felt a sharp pain as the bright light overwhelmed him. Gradually, starting to become aware of the sounds around him. Still struggling to identify a familiar voice, he thought he heard. But whose voice was it?

The recognition of a voice alone brought hope, possibly a false hope, but a hope nonetheless. Falling back asleep was the only option available. Still, while doing so, Anthony felt more assured despite needing more time to distinguish between a virtual world and reality.

Waking once again as the sounds people muttered began to become more recognizable, words forming becoming meaningful phrases, taking words in their usual or most basic sense to have meaning now.

"Welcome back, stranger, and you scared me half to death, Anthony."

Anthony was conscious, but not too coherent, still remaining unsure of anything present.

"Where am I?"

Not waiting for a reply, "Is your horse all right?"

Anthony needed to hear no more words to confirm where he might be now. Sensing Celeste's presence and the warmth of her tears on his cheek was sheer ecstasy.

"It's me, Celeste, and you're in the hospital, Anthony, recovering. You're going to be fine, Anthony; trust me, you'll be fine."

Anthony's throbbing head and entire body hurt as he tries to focus despite his blurred vision. Being somewhat aware of all of the medical apparatus seemingly connected to him everywhere, with their steady beeping, all these pieces of hospital equipment only added confusion to the moment's anxiety as he asked.

"Recovering?"

He still looked confused and disoriented, needing help speaking, never clearly.

"How long have I been here?"

Anthony continues to struggle while in a confusing, insecure, foggy state.

"Why am I here? Was there an accident?"

Anthony became aware enough of his surroundings, now assured that he was speaking with Celeste, not Pati'na.

"Anthony, can you recall anything, anything at all?"

Celeste waited patiently, hoping to see any indication that Anthony was becoming more aware of the situation.

Becoming increasingly irritated, Anthony said, "I don't remember much, Celeste,"

When he tried moving, he immediately felt discomfort.

"I don't understand what's happening, and my head is throbbing."

He trailed off, holding his head and noticing an issue with his hand.

"I'm not sure if any of this is real or…How did I hurt my hand?"

Celeste noticed Dr. Kilpatrick had entered the room and indicated it was time to give Anthony some rest and much-needed sleep, as he was still fighting for survival.

Giving his hand a gentle squeeze, Celeste said, "You've been through a lot in the past few days, Anthony. Your doctor needs me to leave now so you can sleep. We'll be nearby and will visit you once the doctor's permission allows, Anthony."

As Celeste exited Anthony's room, she felt more assured, sensing a relief that he would survive while on her way to meet Teddy and Vienna to relay her conversation before parting for the evening.

Teddy returned to his hospital while Vienna and Celeste hailed a cab to return to their nearby hotel to freshen up before heading out for a meal and a much-needed and a little stress-free, more relaxing evening.

Teddy phoned, saying Dr. Kilpatrick had called to confirm that everything overnight had proceeded as hoped. Anthony continued to sleep well while remaining stable. Visitation would only be allowed once she decided it was safe to do so. They could visit the hospital if need be, but not enter Anthony's room, disturbing him.

The next few days continued to drag on, with every second feeling like an eternity as they waited each day to receive word on Anthony's progress.

Teddy called as Dr. Kilpatrick had notified him that things had improved to the point where Anthony could now receive family visitors, two at a time.

Teddy followed Celeste into the room, and at long last, Anthony struggled to display that famous grin he was well known for.

"We have quite a story to tell you if you think you're up to it, Anthony, or would you rather that we wait a little longer?"

Celeste's outstretched arms reached out, desperately wanting to hug Anthony warmly.

"I probably should wait, Celeste, but I'm so happy to be with you and don't want to close my eyes to find out this could only be a dream."

Still out of Anthony's view, Teddy pulled up a chair near Anthony.

"I would like to know what happened, Celeste, and needless to say, if I fall asleep, it'll have to wait, but I am curious about what happened."

Nodding in agreement, Celeste continued, "This whole thing started several nights ago when, as usual, we had all planned and gathered together with our friends at the Culture Center for another evening of just getting together, having fun, and then enjoying some journeying.”

“Looking back now, you mentioned, and more than once, I think, that you weren’t feeling like yourself that evening. I should have picked up on it then, but regrettably, I didn’t.”

Anthony reached out, indicating things happen sometimes.

“Before we started the journey, a new member, one you befriended last month, showed us a bowl he had created while taking some lessons in woodturning.”

“I do remember that you mentioned it.”

“You were pretty impressed, not so much by the bowl itself, but with the beautiful patina on the bowl. Then, just as Doug took back his bowl, you appeared to become weak, much paler, and kind of gasping for air, clutching your chest. It was so apparent that you were experiencing acute agonizing pain while clutching your chest, limpness, collapsing, as you fell to the floor with your wrist smashing the edge of the old marble table. I panicked, literally scared to death, screaming for help. Luckily, two medical professionals were part of our group that night, Dr. Williams and LPN Margo, who quickly administered CPR on you.”

“They prevented things from getting more chaotic than they already were and started dictating tasks for us to do and ensuring we told them when we had them done. They were terrific! Vienna immediately called 911, and shortly, an ambulance was whisking you off to the hospital as we followed behind in my car.”

Seeing ‘that’ look of disapproval on Anthony’s face, Celeste added, “I know, Anthony. I know I shouldn’t have been driving. Once they had you stabilized and out of immediate danger, Dr. Schwartz, the emergency doctor, spoke with Teddy and me, saying that you had suffered acute, severe, non-repairable damage to your heart and were now desperately in need of a transplant. Then Dr. Walters, the Lead of the Heart Transplant Team, took Teddy aside, speaking to him directly.”

“A heart had been made available from a donor who succumbed this evening in an automobile accident just two hours before, and this heart was available if Teddy made an immediate decision. Teddy signed the required hospital documents for your heart transplant, Anthony, and the never-ending waiting began. I've never been so scared in my entire life, Anthony. How mortal we all are. I can't imagine any life without you. I was terrified, so afraid of losing you. And what a blessing and relief it was to have Teddy here with me."

Anthony tried looking for Teddy.

"Is Teddy here?"

"Teddy never left, Anthony, preferring to remain in the hospital for the entire time, sleeping here overnight in the Family Room for the past few nights until you were now in a more stable condition."

Celeste stood, allowing Teddy to take her chair. Teddy came into Anthony's view with his eyes narrating his emotional pent-up anxiety, taking controlled breaths, releasing stored fears and regrets, then began;

"This has been an eye-opening experience for me these last few days, Anthony, in so very many ways, some rather embarrassing. Celeste's call terrified me. I never felt so useless, so helpless before. You, my dear brother, are most fortunate to have this amazing young woman, Celeste, in your life. Anthony, over the years, almost on a daily basis, I have someone's life in my hands. This might have given me a false sense of being immune to the emotional aspect always present in these cases."

Teddy looks away, wiping his eyes dry.

"But this night, the night when Celeste called in distress, I became simply a brother whose younger brother was in need of a miracle. I so often became that miracle worker. That night, I became that nerd trying to ride your bike, useless."

"It was Celeste who grasped my situation with me trying to deal with the present while combating my past demons from our childhood, where so often I was never there for you, and it was apparent that once again I wasn't going to be there for you, there were several moments where my ineptness was wasting time, with precious seconds ticking away. Celeste was the one who steadied my bearing, making sure that I made the right decisions. Celeste, not me."

Anthony grew increasingly tired and eventually closed his eyes. As he drifted off, he experienced a clear vision: an angel riding a horse with no legs, which turned out to be his red-tailed hawk. This journey was not the usual experience, different than any he had taken before, more like hallucinating as strong medications induced it.

Celeste's welcoming, nervous laughter broke the solemnity of the moment. Wanting to do anything that would give her cause and prevent her from bursting into tears again, she turned toward Anthony.

"Oh, I can't tell you how relieved I am that you are still here with us, Anthony, with this fantastic gift of life from your donor, your precious second chance."

Celeste, looking around, asking, "Can I get you something, Anthony?"

"Would you like a glass of water or something?"

"A glass of water, but only if it's wet."

"Only if it's wet."

"That's mad, Anthony. Now that's the silly mad Anthony, I remember."

# Epilogue

As anticipated, Anthony fully recovered. Dr. Edward Rodgers was his best man, escorting Vienna, Celeste's maid of honor, to Celeste's and Anthony's wedding at the Morishburg Community Culture Center.

The venue was adorned with vibrant summer flowers, and the air was filled with excitement and relief. The ceremony took place on a splendid summer's day in late July, with the sun casting a warm glow on the couple as they exchanged their vows.

And then, as life often surprises us, Teddy's path crossed with Cynthia's, his soulmate, on a day that would change their lives forever.

Three years later, Cynthia Artemis and Dr. Edward Rodgers exchanged marital vows. There was one significant addition to the wedding party: Cynthia asked Celeste if their young daughter could be their flower girl.

As people arrived at the appointed time and place, a hush escorted the wedding party's entrance to the delight of their friends and family gathered that day. The guests, dressed in their finest attire, watched with bated breath as the wedding party descended the aisle. Leading the wedding party's entrance was the prettiest of flower girls, Anthony and Celeste's daughter, Pati'na, who charmed everyone with her innocence and grace.

9 7 9 8 8 9 1 5 5 7 6 0 4